The STORYTELLER

V. Ben Kendrick

FOREWORD by Dr. C. Raymond Buck
INTRODUCTION by Dr. Paul Dixon

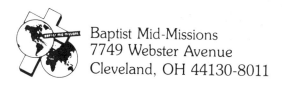

Baptist Mid-Missions
7749 Webster Avenue
Cleveland, OH 44130-8011

© 1986 Baptist Mid-Missions
Printed for Baptist Mid-Missions
by
REGISTER GRAPHICS
220 Main Street
Randolph, NY 14772
ISBN 0-941645-00-2

Acknowledgement

I wish to express my appreciation to Sallie McElwain for her excellent work in typing, proofreading and numerous other helps in the preparation of this manuscript. A special thanks is given to Lynne Tanner who also helped with the typing and proofreading.

THE STORYTELLER

(A Collection of Short Stories)

Foreword

Dr. V. Ben Kendrick has gained a well-deserved recognition as Baptist Mid-Missions' super storyteller. I am pleased to be able to add a few words to the most recent example of his eye for the exciting and his instinct for the inspiring.

In former years, Dr. Kendrick and I walked together on the path of missionary service he describes in his stories. We were co-workers in the Central African Republic, and we continued that for many more years at Baptist Mid-Missions' office. In addition to that, we have been <u>friends</u> throughout these many years.

Missionary children in Africa, and young people by the thousands in the United States and Canada have a special name for Dr. Kendrick. To them, he is "Uncle Ben." You are certain to receive a blessing and an exciting experience as you look at the mission field, through the eyes of Uncle Ben.

> *C. Raymond Buck, Ph.D., President Emeritus*
> *Baptist Mid-Missions*

Table of Contents

1 The Destroyed Altar 19
2 Almost Cut Off 23
3 The Whole Town Turned Out 26
4 Just a Piece of Iron 30
5 Dr. Benson's Plan 35
6 Rain From Heaven 40
7 The First Opportunity 43
8 God In Every Detail 46
9 My Heart Sings 50
10 Struck By Lightning 54
11 The God That Lost Its Head 57
12 God Was in the Wind 62
13 Ten Long Years 67
14 Good News from Ngende 72
15 God Turned Him Around 76
16 Never Too Busy 80
17 Did God Do Something? 84
18 A Concrete Answer 89
19 The Dogwood Tree 93
20 Jim's Mission Field 96
21 Just In Time 101
22 One Lone White Duck 105
23 New Truth 108
24 Starting All Over 113
25 That One Cookie 117
26 His Way is Best 121
27 God's Appointments 125
28 Tracks in the Snow 130
29 Safe at Home 133
30 Not In Vain 138
31 Doli's Sacrifice 142

Dedication

It is with thanksgiving that I dedicate this book to three church families which have played an important part in my life—Bible Baptist Church, Shickshinny, Pennsylvania; North Baptist Church, Rochester, New York; and Cedar Hill Baptist Church, Cleveland Heights, Ohio.

Introduction

Ben Kendrick is very special to me. This premier missionary along with his wife, Nina, gave 21 years of faithful, soul winning service on foreign fields. Ben has served as a traveling representative for Baptist Mid-Missions, reaching into churches and among Christians nationwide with the burden he has for missionary endeavors.

People who know Ben realize that God has poured into his life a wealth of rich, missionary experiences—some of which are truly miraculous. It is to God's glory that He has also gifted this servant to be able to communicate these stimulating stories through both biographical and fictional writing.

This book is yet another exciting selection of short stories from our brother. He has a singular way of making missionary accounts come to life. Also included in this book are non-missionary stories—just as entertaining and meaningful.

This book will provoke you to laughter and perhaps draw some tears. It will convict you of your shortcomings and motivate in you a commitment to aggressive witness and discipleship efforts. In short, be prepared to be a better person upon completion of *The Storyteller.*

Dr. Paul Dixon, President
Cedarville College

About
the
Author

V. Ben Kendrick was born in Shickshinny, a small town in northeast Pennsylvania. When Ben was fourteen years of age, his family moved to northern New Jersey. There he graduated in 1946 from Pompton Lakes High School. He attended and graduated from Baptist Bible College of Pennsylvania (formerly Baptist Bible Seminary, Johnson City, New York). He has served that institution as a Trustee and as President of the Alumni Association. In 1949 Rev. Kendrick was accepted by Baptist Mid-Missions and served with his wife Nina for 21 years in the Chad and Central African Republics. In 1973 he joined the staff of the Mission, serving as Deputation Administrator. Denver Baptist Bible College honored Rev. Kendrick with a Doctor of Divinity degree in 1980.

This is Dr. Kendrick's sixth book. Previous books are *Buried Alive for Christ, Battle for Yanga, Flight From Death, A World of Treasure* (co-authored with Nina Kendrick) and *Yanga, The Miracle Village.*

1
The
Destroyed
Altar

The crude-looking altar caught Walt's eye. Placed neatly on top of it were three ears of corn and a small yam. The veteran missionary stopped on the jungle path and turned to his African companions.

"Tell me, Andrew," said the inquisitive missionary to one of the men, "why do your people make offerings like this? I've been living here among you twelve years now and I'm sure there is far more to these altars than I know."

As Walt spoke, he pointed at the two-foot high structure just a step off the side of the path. The altar consisted of four sticks in the ground with a small platform built on top. It's crude appearance caused Walt to believe it had been built in a hurry.

The other six men stood in silence as the local church deacon spoke with their American missionary friend. The rays of the morning sun filtered through the overhanging trees illustrating the rippled tribal scars on the Christian's face. In his close relationship with the tribe's believers, Walt had often heard the terrible accounts of the tribal ceremonies when the young men and women received their scars. Each year there were those who did not return from the devil worship rites. Their bodies would be buried in shallow jungle graves—the effects of the cuttings and beatings were just too much to survive.

"It's interesting that you ask me about this, Mr. Warner," answered the church leader. "I happen to know the background on this one."

The men sat down as Andrew began his story.

"Several nights ago a woman was walking on this path after dark. You know our people well enough, Mr. Warner, that they are very fearful of the night. If they can help it at all, they will not go out after dark."

Walt nodded his head in agreement. He had heard many stories about the fears and beliefs of the dark African nights. Andrew continued.

"She was walking by this very spot where we are when she saw a person standing right there." The deacon pointed to where the altar was located.

"You say she saw a . . . a . . . person, Andrew?" questioned Walt.

"That's right," answered the African. "She saw a person. My people call it an 'evil spirt'—and they are always white, Mr. Warner."

"What did she do when she saw this . . . 'evil spirit'?" asked Walt.

"Well, she knew there was only one thing for her to do—build an altar and make an offering as soon as possible on this very spot. You see, Mr. Warner, the unsaved people of our tribe believe that this 'evil spirit' will bring sickness and even death to the family of the one who sees it if that person doesn't make a sacrifice immediately."

"I see," said Walt, slowly shaking his head. "So she really built the altar and made the offerings to protect herself and her family?"

"That's correct," responded Andrew. "And she did it that same night, too. She ran to her village which is about a mile from here, got her machete and cut the sticks you see there. She put the offerings on the altar as soon as it was built."

"Did she see the 'person' again?" asked Walt of his friend.

"No, she didn't," answered Andrew. "When she came back, it had gone. She will keep offerings on this altar for the next twelve moons."

Walt sat in silence as he thought of what Andrew had just told him. There were many questions that popped into his mind but the whereabouts of the woman was foremost in his thinking.

"Do you know where the woman is now, Andrew?" he asked soberly.

"I think she's in her cotton garden," answered one of the other men. "She is the wife of my cousin and I know them well. She is a very wicked woman, Mr. Warner. Her house is filled with witchcraft items."

"Let's go find her, Andrew," demanded the missionary. "The Lord has placed her on my heart and I want to talk with her."

The group of men started down the path toward the distant village. A short time later they came to a fork in the path.

"Her garden is on this path," spoke the woman's relative.

The men did not walk very far before they came upon a cotton garden. At the side of the garden was a woman partially hidden among the plants. She was busily picking the fluffy white balls.

"There she is, Mr. Warner," offered Andrew, pointing to the distant lone figure. Walt motioned for Andrew and the woman's relative to go with him.

"The rest of you men wait here for us," said Walt. "The three of us will go and talk with her."

"Hello, there," called the missionary as he and the two men approached the woman. "We thought we would stop and talk with you a bit."

The startled woman stood up with a jerk. Walt could see fear written all over her face.

"Don't be afraid, Sousou," said her relative. "Mr. Warner saw your altar up the path and he asked me to bring him to you. He has some good news to tell you."

Seeing her relative, Sousou walked over to Walt and shook his hand.

"Thank you for coming. What good news do you have for me?"

"I heard you saw an 'evil spirit' the other night and how you made that altar for it. I saw, too, the offerings you put on it."

"That's what happened," answered Sousou. "I hope I'm safe now from all those terrible things that could happen to me and my family."

"What things are you talking about, Sousou?" asked the curious missionary.

"Well, the worst thing that could happen would be for any of us to die. We're afraid of death. Our ancestors have told us that we can persuade the evil spirit to keep death away if we are faithful in making sacrifices and giving offerings."

"But won't the wild animals eat your offerings and sacrifices?" asked Walt, looking puzzled.

"Oh, yes!" replied Sousou. "They will but they're controlled by the evil spirit, too. You see, the evil spirit doesn't get angry with them. It only gets angry with people."

Walt's heart ached for the woman. It was difficult for him to even imagine the terrible fear which held her captive.

"I know of a sacrifice that nothing can destroy," said Walt with a smile.

"You do?" responded Sousou, somewhat surprised to hear of such a sacrifice.

"Yes, I do, Sousou," answered Walt. "The sacrifice I'm talking about is all powerful. In fact, His name is Jesus. He's the Son of God—the God we men love and serve."

"But. . .but, why do you love Him? How do you serve Him? I. . .I. . .don't understand," said Sousou, looking bewildered.

"Let me tell you about Him," said Walt. "It's an amazing story and the wonderful thing about it is that it is all true."

As the men listened, Walt explained how Christ came and died on the cross as the supreme sacrifice for man's sins. He told about heaven and how those who accept God the Father's sacrifice go there to live forever. When he spoke about hell, Sousou grimaced with fear.

"Jesus can take away all your fear, Sousou. He is much more powerful than all the evil spirits. He will protect you from the great evil one, too."

"I want your Jesus, White Man," said Sousou, taking a step closer. "How do I get to know Him like you do?"

"You can ask Him, right here—right now, to forgive you of all your wicked ways and to give you everlasting life. He'll do that for you, Sousou. All you have to do is ask Him."

As the men listened, the once wicked woman confessed her sins and asked Jesus to save her. Her face shone with happiness when she finished praying. The three men shook her hand. They headed for the group of men waiting on the far side of the garden.

"I feel good inside, White Man. I've never felt so clean and happy before," said the new convert.

"You are God's child now, Sousou," spoke up Andrew.

After shaking hands with the rest of the men, Sousou started up the path.

"Where are you going?" asked her relative, following close behind her.

"To the altar," she laughed. "I'm going to show the 'evil spirit' that it can't hurt me. I have Jesus now."

The group of excited believers headed for the altar which would soon be destroyed—a testimony of a new creation in Christ Jesus.

(Reprinted by permission of Regular Baptist Press)

2
Almost
Cut
Off
(Based on a true experience)

The blow from the machete caught Ganda on the wrist. The terrified boy looked at his nearly severed hand. The nearby thrashing antelope caught in the hunting net gained a temporary reprieve as the hunters' attention was drawn to their seriously wounded friend.

"Stop the bleeding!" shouted one of the men as he raced to Ganda's side. The young African sat dazed while the blood spurted from the huge, open gash.

Within seconds another man had quickly removed his shirt and torn off one of the sleeves. He tied the two ends together and slipped it over Ganda's arm just above the elbow. He then took a short stick, inserted it into the crude tourniquet and turned it to put pressure on the arm.

"I saw my father do this when my uncle cut his leg chopping wood one time," he said with a proud look on his face. The others stood looking on with amazement as the flow of blood reduced to a drop now and then.

"We have to take him to the hospital," said one of the hunters. "Only the doctor can help Ganda now. Otherwise he will die."

"But that is a four hour walk," spoke Ganda. "I might lose all my blood by then."

"No, you won't lose all your blood," responded the shirtless African. "I'll keep this band tight so you won't bleed."

Ten of the men prepared to take Ganda to the hospital while the others remained at the hunting site to care for the nets and captured animals. Several men hurriedly prepared a crude stretcher from poles and bark strips.

On her way from the children's classes, Alice Peters stopped in at the hospital to check on a patient. The missionary nurse was just mounting her bicycle when she saw the group of men enter the hospital driveway. As she hurried toward the approaching men, Alice noticed that some were dressed in animal skins while others wore simple loin cloths.

"They come from deep in the bush," she whispered to herself.

Arriving alongside the stretcher, Alice saw the great amount of blood stains. She quickly called for one of her African helpers and sent him running to Dr. Rand's house with the urgent message for him to come immediately.

The teenage boy was already in the x-ray room when Dr. Rand arrived to take pictures of the injured arm. The cuff tourniquet was inflated to enable the missionary doctor to make the necessary examination.

"The major bones are intact, Alice," spoke Dr. Rand. "But we have a major repair job to do. Thank the Lord that the main artery is not cut."

With the IV's started, blood typed and antibiotics and premedication given, Dr. Rand ordered the operating room to be readied. Alice and two African nurses, Andrew and Mark, quickly prepared for the long, delicate surgery which would soon take place.

"This boy comes from Ouaka, Dr. Rand," said Mark as he entered the scrub room with the doctor. "That is the village where Pastor Timothy went to start a work last year and was chased out by the chief."

"Yes, I remember that, Mark. The chief's name is Bando and he is the one who also works closely with the witchdoctor."

"That's right," responded the Christian nurse. "He has been known to practice a lot of witchcraft himself."

Mark motioned toward the operating room. "Ganda is the chief's grandson. His father just told me that as soon as Bando hears what has happened, he will come to the hospital to be with Ganda."

Throughout the seven hours of surgery, the mission doctor was conscious of all that hung in the balance with the operation. "Lord," he prayed after completing the surgery, "give Ganda the use of his hand again. And, Father, I pray that he will accept you as Savior. Father, open up the village of Ouaka to the gospel."

Before he left the hospital to return to his house, Dr. Rand stopped to see his latest patient. Ganda awoke to find the doctor standing over him.

"Hello, Ganda," spoke Dr. Rand in his kind voice. "The operation went well. You'll have some pain for several days, but it will pass. And don't worry, we'll take good care of you here."

"Where is he? Where is my grandson?" The loud voice coming from the hall caused Ganda and the doctor to look toward the door. At that moment, a tall, ugly, scar-faced African came rushing into the room.

"There you are," shouted the man as he rushed to Ganda's bed. "Are you all right, my child? Have they done you any harm?"

"I'm all right, Grandfather," responded the lad. "Dr. Rand sewed my hand back on. Even our gods can't do that."

Ganda's face reflected the seriousness of the boy's remarks. The African chief seemed stunned. "Don't talk like that, Ganda," the chief rebuked. "Our gods will get angry and you'll lose your hand."

"But we need to learn about the doctor's God, Grandfather. All the workers here know about Him. They talk to Him like they really know Him."

That night the chief made his way to Dr. Rand's house. The two men sat on the veranda and talked for over an hour. Finally Chief Bando stood up to leave.

"I must go back to Ganda, Dr. Rand. Thank you for telling me about your God. I will give your words much thought. Good night, Dr. Rand."

The chief took a few steps, stopped and turned around. "And if my grandson's hand gets well, then I will know that your God is stronger than my gods. I'll even ask you to come to my village, Dr. Rand, and tell my people about your Jesus."

Dr. Rand felt good as he watched the chief go down the path. He believed in his heart that within a short time, a very short time, he would have the joy of preaching the gospel of Christ in the village of Ouaka, which had almost been cut off.

(Reprinted by permission of Regular Baptist Press)

3
The
Whole Town
Turned Out

"**I** want you and Nina to come back home. I want the whole town to know that we are sending out our first missionaries to the mission field."

Hearing those words from my beloved pastor, Rev. A.F. Birdsall, sent the chills rippling through my body. The man sitting before me in his wheel chair knew me like his own son. His influence in my life seemed to touch upon every major decision that I made in my teenage years. His love for me was unquestionable.

I recalled how, growing up as a boy in Shickshinny, Pennsylvania, I looked upon Pop Birdsall as the man who was able to come up with the right answers at the right time. He was the leading spiritual influence in that small eastern Pennsylvania town of 2,500 people.

As I stood there looking at this outstanding Christian statesman, I marveled at what God had done through him over the few years that I had known him. Just the fact that he pastored the little white church on Furnace Street from a wheel chair for thirty years was a milestone accomplishment in itself.

"Did you say, Pop, that you want the whole town to know? How are you going to do that?" I asked placing my hand on his shoulder.

"You just leave that up to me, Ben. There is nothing too big that I won't tackle for my God. That'll be no problem. You just come back home and let me give you and Nina a real send-off." I could see the twinkle in Pop's eyes as he spoke.

"What a man," I thought to myself. "What a wonderful man of God."

I remembered how my parents moved from Shickshinny to northern New Jersey where Dad found work. Even there, Pop continued to have an influence in my life. There was that summer when I worked at a youth camp in the Pocono Mountains near East Stroudsburg, Pennsylvania. Pop's oldest son, Warren, had graduated from Baptist Bible Seminary in Johnson City, New York, and had taken a small pastorate in Patterson, New Jersey, where I had become a member. Little did I realize that a telephone conversation between son, Warren, and Pop, early one morning would change the course of my life.

"Dad," said Warren, "I'm concerned about Ben. The Lord has laid him upon my heart and I think I'll drive up to camp today and talk with him about going to Bible school."

"Well, son," replied Pop, "why don't you drive in and pick me up? We'll go up together to see Ben."

"That's fine with me, Dad. I'll be along in about three hours. It'll be a long day but I believe God may use us to give Ben direction for his life."

As I was working in the camp kitchen that day, I didn't realize that two of my dearest friends on earth were winding their way through the mountains on their way to speak with me about my preparation for the Lord's work.

"There's someone to see you, Ben," called one of the high school fellows working with me in the kitchen.

"Warren!" I half shouted, "where did you come from?" There was my pastor looking through the screen door from the back steps.

"Dad and I came to talk with you, Ben. Can you come now or do you still have work to do?"

"I've just finished. Where's Pop?"

"He's in the car over there," he answered, pointing to the black shiny vehicle at the end of the building.

Within minutes we were driving along a mountain road. Pop and Warren told me how the Lord had burdened their hearts for me and that they came to talk with me about going to Bible school that Fall. I glanced at Warren who was only a few years my senior. A serious but pleasant look was on his face.

"But, Pop," I said, "I haven't even sent in an application. I don't think there's time to start this fall."

"You just leave everything up to me, Ben. I'll get you an application to fill out but we won't worry about that now. I'll see that you're accepted. You have to tell the Lord you'll go first."

"Dear Father," I prayed in the car, "thank You for sending these two men to talk with me today. I will take their advice and go to Bible school. I accept what they have to say as from You."

Now several years later, that blessed day flashed before me as I stood once again beside Pop sitting in his wheel chair. I was nearing graduation from Bible school and once more listened to that familiar voice.

"Praise God, Ben, for your call to Africa. I can guarantee you, son, that the church will stand behind you in prayer and financial support." Up to that time, the church did not have a missions program and had never really supported a missionary on a regular basis. The tears swelled up in my eyes as he spoke.

"You and Nina go and meet Baptist Mid-Missions' Council as planned. After you are accepted, I want to do something special for you here in your home town." Pop spoke with that determined look on his face. I felt the excitement once again ripple through my body as I listened. I looked at Pop sitting there waiting for my answer.

"Whatever you say, Pop. If you want Nina and me to come back home to Shickshinny, we'll do it. Just give me the dates."

Pop Birdsall did just what he said he would do. There wasn't a thing that he would not attempt to do for the Lord. If he wanted the whole town to know about their first missionaries leaving for the field, he would do it.

He ran an article with a large picture in the town's newspaper, The Mountain Echo. He also ran a story in the papers of two nearby cities, Wilkes-Barre and Berwick.

I remember so well the day we arrived in Shickshinny and I asked Pop about his plans.

"Well," he said with that half grin on his face, "The Pennsylvania State Police and the town policeman will block off all traffic coming into town. The schools will be closed for the parade which will be led by the high school band. You will ride with me in the mayor's car and we will have a farewell service in the town square."

As usual, I stood in utter amazement as he spoke and unfolded his fantastic plans.

"Man," I said, "what a great day for the testimony of the Lord here in Shickshinny."

Pop reached out and patted me on my hand. "We're doing it for Him, Ben. I'm not afraid to ask for anything as long as it's for the

Lord and His glory." I knew Pop meant what he said.

"You are really something else, Pop," I said, thrilled that I was a part of this outstanding event in my home town.

The sound of the band music could be heard approaching. Pop was lifted from his wheel chair and placed in the front seat of the mayor's convertible. Nina and I, with our two year old daughter, Pam, occupied the back seat. Two large colorful banners were fastened to each side of the car. They read, "BEN, NINA AND PAM, AFRICA BOUND."

The convertible lined up behind the band and we made our way slowly down to the main street which ran the entire length of the town. All traffic came to a halt as the parade proceeded through the small community.

"This is a great day for the Lord's work in Shickshinny, Ben," called Pop from the front seat as he waved to the crowd lining each side of Main Street. I could almost see the joy bubbling out of him. The parade stopped in the center of town where a loud speaker was set up for the farewell service.

I can still see Pop as he spoke into the microphone. "This is a memorable day in the history of Shickshinny," he said. "We are sending forth our first missionaries who will carry the Gospel of Jesus Christ to the land of Africa."

What a joy it was for me to tell my home town people how God had saved me and called me to serve Him as a missionary.

After Warren closed that unusual service in prayer, I looked at Pop. A crooked smile spread across his face.

"You were right, Pop," I said. "The whole town has turned out."

(Reprinted by permission of Regular Baptist Press)

4
Just
a Piece
of Iron

Banda muttered his discontentment as he rolled over on his grass mat.

"Who do they think they are, beating that iron so early in the morning? Don't they know there are people trying to sleep around here?"

The village blacksmith stuck a finger in each ear to shut out the sounds of the clanging iron. Sunday mornings were always greeted by the beating of the 'church bell' by the old guard at the mission station up on top of the hill.

Banda had been an adversary to the missionaries' work for years. Still fresh in the minds of the local residents was his attempt to set fire to the grass roof of the church building. The church was located on the edge of the mission concession near the forests. One of the station workmen had spotted Banda just in time as he approached the church with the fire.

"I'll stop this nonsense somehow," spoke the blacksmith to himself. "Fools! That's what they are—crazy fools, to believe such ridiculous lies about that Book and the missionaries' God."

The irate African got out of bed and walked to the door of his hut. Enraged, he shook his fist toward the mission station on the hill.

"You'll hear from me, you Jesus lovers. I'll get you yet."

Banda set about to prepare his breakfast. Because of his vicious, ill-tempered ways, his wife and children had fled from his house. This made him even meaner. Most of the men in the village had had a fight with him at one time or another. His drunkened activities were well known throughout the area. The angry blacksmith went about making his morning coffee. As he worked, a plan slowly developed in his heart.

"That iron," he whispered to himself, "I'll steal their iron."

As he though of his plan, a sneer spread across his scarred face. Banda spit on the floor to show his hatred for the missionaries and the national believers.

Later that morning he sat in front of his hut as the Christians walked by on their way to church. The few who greeted Banda received a blank stare in response. In no way did Banda want to contaminate himself with those who worshipped the missionaries' God.

The sound of their singing voices soon drifted down to the village. Banda looked around to make sure no one was watching and then cupped his hand by his ear to catch the words of the hymn.

"What can wash away my sins? Nothing but the blood of Jesus.
What can make me whole again? Nothing but the blood of Jesus."

"The blood of Jesus?" he whispered. "What makes that Man any different from me? Why do they have to sing about Him that way?"

Kicking at a small stool as he stood up, Banda made his way into his hut. He untied the string holding a monkey skull hanging from a bamboo rafter. Carefully he placed the small skull on an altar in the center of the hut. The blacksmith then fell to his knees in front of the crude looking altar and bent forward, touching his forehead to the clay floor.

The monkey god was recognized to be one of the most powerful of all gods. It was the general belief that it was responsible for burning buildings, destroying gardens and causing sickness.

After bowing several times, Banda arose, hoping he had pleased the monkey god. He was ready now to carry out his plan to silence the 'chuch bell' once and for all.

The day passed without any more encounters with the village Christians. The sun had just dropped behind the distant hill. It was time for Banda to head out into the night. He tucked the box of matches in his pocket, fastened his knife to his belt and picked up his two-foot machete. Before blowing out his kerosene lantern, he took a glance at the little skull hanging from the bamboo rafter.

"I'm counting on you to help me," he said, closing the door of his hut.

The blacksmith knew the forests like he knew the inside of his hut.

Quickly but silently he made his way to the edge of the mission station. He looked out from the tall grass to see the church building not more than thirty feet away. Banda looked around to make sure the old guard was no where in sight. He expertly moved out from the grass and headed for the tree where the 'church bell' hung. Quickly he unfastened the wire holding the iron and moved toward the church building. Inside the grass-roof chapel, he took the matches from his pocket. Within seconds, the dry grass began to blaze. By the time the flame was spotted, Banda was back into the forest with the 'church bell' securely under his arm.

Excitement filled the village as the people ran to the fire. Inside his hut, Banda sat rubbing the monkey skull, mumbling his thanks to the monkey god for a successful evening.

The blacksmith got up early the next morning, started his charcoal fire around the stolen piece of iron and pumped hard on the goat skin bellows to heat it. Looking about him to make sure none of the villagers were watching, he took the red hot iron from the fire and heated it over and over again to change its shape as quickly as possible. Banda was relieved when the iron finally lost all resemblance of its previous shape.

"No one will recognize it now," he said to himself.

"Hello, Banda," called one of the men of the village. "You're working early this morning."

The blacksmith looked up from where he sat cross-legged in the small shelter.

"I've got an order for some knives and spears and I want to finish them today," he answered, paying little attention to his questioner.

By mid-morning, the 'church bell' was beaten out into fifteen flat pieces of metal, ready to be shaped into knives and spears. The destruction of the mission station church and the missing 'bell' took the usual onlookers away from the blacksmith shop. Banda tried not to think of the crime he had committed, but the sight and feel of the metal kept it before him. His conscience began to bother him.

"What can wash away my sins? Nothing but the blood of Jesus."

The words of the hymn came to mind.

"Why His blood?" he asked himself. "He's only a man like me. How can His blood wash my sins away? Is He stronger than the monkey god?"

Banda beat harder on the iron.

"I've got to stop thinking about this Man, Jesus," he whispered. "What has He to do with this iron anyway?"

"Hello, Banda!" came the familiar voice from outside the shop.

The busy blacksmith glanced up to see Pastor Mark. Contacts between these two men were few and then it was the pastor who made the approach. Banda kept working as he spoke.

"Hello, Pastor. What brings you to my shop?"

Pastor Mark stooped to enter the low shelter.

"I've come to see if you have a piece of iron to sell to the church. You see, someone stole the church bell last night at the same time as the church burned."

"I. . .I. . .don't have a piece that big now," stammered Banda. "I only had this one piece, which I'm using to make some knives and spears."

"Well, let me know, Banda, when you do find something. Maybe we could pay you to make a real bell for us."

"I. . .I. . .I'll let you know," responded the blacksmith nervously.

The pastor knelt down and picked up one of the pieces of metal. Pretending he was beating a bell, he smiled at the blacksmith.

"You could have the privilege of being the first to beat it, Banda. Would you do that for us?"

Banda turned to his work after the pastor left. Never before had he felt so bad inside. The words of the hymn kept coming back into his thoughts. He picked up a piece of metal and then dropped it to the ground. He could still see the pastor's smile and hear his words.

"They've never done anything mean to me," he muttered. "Why did I burn their church? Why did I do such a thing?"

Within minutes, Banda was on his way to the pastor's house. In his hands were fifteen pieces of metal. A serious look covered his face. He found Pastor Mark sitting outside by the fire.

"Pastor," said the blacksmith, his voice quivering. "I've come to tell you the truth."

The surprised pastor stood to welcome his visitor.

"What do you mean, Banda?"

"I stole your church iron. I burned the church building. I did it, Pastor!"

The two men stood in silence looking at each other. Finally Banda spoke.

"I know it's just a piece of metal, Pastor, but your God has been troubling me over it. I have to get right with Him and the Christians."

"There's only one way to do that, Banda," spoke Pastor Mark. "That is to accept Jesus as your Savior. Confess your sins and He'll save you. He'll give you eternal life."

The two men went inside the pastor's house where they knelt together. The blacksmith confessed his sins and asked Christ to save him. After his conversion, Banda talked with the pastor, asking many questions. A short time later they came out of the house. Banda bent over and picked up the pieces of iron.

"Here's the start for our church bell, Pastor," he smiled as he spoke. "Like I said, it was just a piece of iron, but God used it to bring me to Jesus."

"Yes, He did, Banda," added Pastor Mark, "and this is just the beginning for you . . . just the beginning."

(Reprinted by permission of Regular Baptist Press)

5
Dr.
Benson's
Plan

Mary looked out the window to see two men walk by. Balanced on each of their shoulders were two six foot poles. Lying limp in a blanket connecting the poles was an Indian woman. Following close behind the men walked a small boy carrying handmade crutches.

The missionary nurse hurried to the open door just in time to see the men place their human cargo on the floor. Mary recognized the woman as Nabu, a resident of a nearby village.

"What happened to her?" Mary asked, bending down to feel the Indian woman's pulse.

"She became ill two days ago," responded one of the men. "When she stopped talking to us we decided to bring her to you."

Nabu was burning with fever. Mary called to one of the Indian hospital helpers.

"Matthew! Run quickly and get Dr. Benson. Tell him that Nabu is unconscious."

The worker immediately left running. Everyone in the area knew Nabu. She was respected by all and looked upon as the mother of her village.

In minutes Mary had the unconscious woman on one of the hospital beds. Dr. Benson came as quickly as possible and went immediately to the bedside of the new patient.

"I think it's malaria," he said after a few minutes. "We'll get a blood smear to make sure. In the meantime, I'll give her an anti-malaria injection."

By the next morning Nabu was much improved. The laboratory

report confirmed the doctor's diagnosis. At noon she asked for something to eat.

"That's a good sign," said the missionary doctor. "She's on the mend now. When the appetite returns, it usually means the patient is feeling better."

Mary took their elderly patient a bowl of chicken broth. Nabu smiled when she saw the nurse approach.

"You are very kind to me," she said, reaching out to touch Mary's arm with her bony fingers. "How can I ever thank you?"

"We would be very happy, Nabu, if you would accept Jesus as your Savior," responded Mary. "Many times you have heard about Him. Don't you think it's time you receive Him?"

Nabu's face took on a serious look.

"When my body is sick, your medicine can make it well. But my head is different. Your medicine can't make that well."

"Oh, it can," said Mary. "Jesus can help you believe, Nabu. He really can! Nothing is too hard for Him to do."

"No," answered the sad-faced woman. "My head can't be made well. It won't allow my heart to believe."

That night Mary shared with her co-workers, Dr. and Mrs. Benson, the conversation she had had with Nabu.

"We must pray for her," said Ruth Benson. "God is able to break down the barriers and touch her heart."

Before she left to go to her house, Mary joined the Benson's in a time of prayer.

"Father," prayed Mary, "please help Nabu to believe. Give us just the right words to say to her."

During the next two days, the elderly woman continued to improve. Both Mary and Dr. Benson witnessed to her but it was always the same answer.

"I can't believe. My head doesn't allow my heart to receive Jesus."

The more the missionaries witnessed to the woman, the more Nabu claimed it was impossible for her to believe because her 'sick' head blocked the good words from reaching her heart.

"If Jesus could make my head well like He did the rest of my body," she told Mary the day before she was to leave the hospital, "then my heart would receive Jesus."

That night Mary was again invited to the Benson home for dinner. In the course of conversation, the subject of Nabu came up.

"I fitted Nabu today for new crutches," said Dr. Benson. "You were home for lunch, Mary, when I did it. I'm surprised she didn't say something to you about it."

"She probably would have but I guess I didn't give her the opportunity. I had to make my rounds this afternoon and when I stopped to talk with her, I told her how much we wanted her to accept Jesus as her Savior."

"What did she say?" asked Ruth.

"She didn't say anything," responded Mary. "She only pointed to her head."

"I don't know of any patient to whom we have witnessed more than Nabu," added Dr. Benson. "I don't know of another thing we can say or do."

"Pray," spoke up Mary. "We can still pray."

Before Mary left the three friends again knelt in the living room and prayed for the salvation of Nabu. Tears came to Mary's eyes as she thought of the little old lady leaving the hospital still lost.

"Good morning, Mary," called Dr. Benson as he met the nurse on her way to the hospital. "Before we discharge Nabu, I want to try something I thought of last night after you left."

"What is it, Dr. Benson?" inquired the nurse.

"A surprise plan, Mary," responded the medical missionary. "Let's go see her now."

Excitement mounted in Mary's heart as she and the doctor approached Nabu's bed. The elderly Indian woman gave her toothless grin when she saw them.

"Bring my new crutches, Doctor," she said, sitting up on the edge of the bed. "I'm going home today."

"Good morning, Nabu," spoke Dr. Benson. "I'll give you your crutches later on in my office. Matthew will take you there in a wheelchair."

The doctor then motioned for Mary to follow him to his office. Once inside, he smiled and pointed to the crutches leaning against the wall.

"Now, we'll wait for Matthew to bring Nabu. I hope my plan works," spoke the physician.

"I hope so, too, Dr. Benson," repeated Mary.

A knock on the door announced the arrival of Matthew with Nabu.

"There are my crutches!" called out Nabu as they entered. "They are right there, Dr. Benson."

"That's correct, Nabu," answered the missionary. He then turned to Mary and Matthew. "Help Nabu to her feet, please."

The elderly woman was assisted to her feet and the doctor pulled the wheelchair away. He then brought the crutches and placed them under Nabu's arms.

"How do they feel, Nabu?" he asked.

"They make a good pair of legs, Dr. Benson. I'll be able to walk everywhere now." Again Nabu showed her toothless grin.

"All right, now lift your arms again, Nabu," requested the doctor.

Obeying his instructions, Nabu raised her arms high. The physician then asked Mary and Matthew to hold her while he removed the crutches. He walked to the other side of the room, turned, and motioned for Nabu to come to him.

"Come to me, Nabu. Come and get your crutches," said the serious-faced doctor.

The old woman helplessly stared at the crutches.

"I . . . I . . . I can't, Dr. Benson. I can't come and get them. I need to lean on them if I go anywhere."

"That's it, Nabu," responded Dr. Benson, smiling. "That's what we have been telling you about Jesus. He will make your head well so your heart can hear. You need to lean on Him."

Nabu's eyes filled with tears as she spoke, her voice trembling with emotion. A tear dropped from her chin.

"I understand, Dr. Benson. I see what you mean. Yes, Jesus can help me and I want to lean on Him."

Nabu hesitated a moment and looked up at the doctor. "Can you help me to lean on Him, Dr. Benson? Can you?"

Seated back in the wheelchair, Nabu prayed, asking God to forgive her of her sins and for Him to save her. When the four friends finally looked at each other, there wasn't a dry eye among them.

Nabu insisted on walking from the hospital, proudly using her new crutches. Outside the entrance she was met by many of her friends. She held up her hand to speak.

"My friends, I have some good words to give you." A hush swept over the crowd that gathered to accompany Nabu back to the village.

"I came here very sick. I could have died, but I'm glad that didn't happen." A low murmur of voices from the crowd indicated their agreement with Nabu's words.

"If I had died, I would have gone to the big fire because I still had my sins and I didn't know Jesus. Today, I learned to lean on Him. I believed in Him and He now lives in my heart. Like I said, I came here sick, but I'm going home well—completely well."

Mary glanced at her co-worker. "Thank the Lord for your plan, Dr. Benson. I must confess you sure had me wondering what you were going to do."

"Yes, thank the Lord," responded the doctor. "A lot of those villagers are going to hear about the Christ that Nabu learned to lean on today."

(Reprinted by permission of Regular Baptist Press)

6
Rain
From
Heaven

The stinging whip cut deep into the flesh on Bama's back. The African youth winced with pain and gripped the pole to which he was lashed. Again and again the buffalo hide whip left its bloody welts on the body of the young Christian.

Satisfied with the beating he had administered, Bama's Uncle Saley turned toward his hut.

"That will teach you to disobey me, you animal. You are fortunate your father is dead. He would have killed you for running away from the Yondo camp."

Bama's mind was numb from the shock of the beating. The suffering teenager slipped to his knees in total exhaustion. He knew that he would not receive any sympathy from the other villagers. He had arrived to live with his uncle and aunt just two months ago. To his disappointment, there was not another Christian in the entire village of Moussa.

To add to Bama's woes, many of his relatives were actively engaged in assisting the area's witchdoctor with the tribe's initiation rites. His uncle at times accompanied the witchdoctor to the jungle camps where the horrible ceremonies took place. Only three years earlier one of Bama's cousins had died from blood poisoning as a result of the many cuts inflicted upon his body for his tribal identification scars.

The youth lifted his head to see his uncle come back out of his hut. The man's face twitched with anger as he approached Bama.

"Get up on your feet, Animal!" he snarled. "No nephew of mine is going to disgrace our family and tribe like you have and live to tell it."

Bama knew his uncle was not given to idle talk. He struggled to his feet only to be knocked back down by a hard blow to his head. The beaten youth lifted his head and spit the dirt from his mouth. Slowly he spoke.

"I . . .I . . .don't want to disobey you, Uncle Saley. I love our family. I'm glad I belong to our tribe." Bama hesitated and then continued, speaking quietly to his adopted father. "I want to be a good Sara tribesman, but . . .I can't go through the Yondo ceremonies. I'm a Christian, Uncle, and my body belongs to. . ."

The young man's voice was silenced by another heavy blow. This one came from a club which knocked him unconscious.

"He's coming out of it now, Saley," one of the men said to Bama's uncle. "I'll throw some more water on him."

Opening his eyes, Bama saw a pile of dirt beside him. His heart leaped with fear as he realized what was happening. He was going to be buried alive. Only a miracle by the Lord would save him. He felt a strange prickling sensation ripple through his body.

"Shall we stand him up, Saley?" asked a man bending down to grab Bama's arm.

"No, just sit him on the edge of the grave. That way we can simply kick him into it if the fool doesn't change his mind about his God."

Bama was only half conscious but he realized what they were doing to him. "Father," he mumbled loud enough for the man nearest him to hear, "please help me to honor Your name."

"Saley, the idiot is still talking to his God. Let's cut his tongue out. That should silence him."

Bama saw the steel blade glimmer in the sunlight. A pair of hands grabbed his face to pry open his mouth.

"Don't do it, Sio!" came the command from Bama's uncle. "Let him call upon his God. I want him to see what a fool he is to waste his time on the One he calls Jesus."

While the men talked among themselves, dark storm clouds suddenly appeared out of nowhere. A loud roll of thunder brought a temporary silence to the group. Large drops of rain began peppering the ground. Saley looked up into the rapidly darkening sky. A sharp crack of lightning sent him along with the other men scurrying for the nearby village.

"But, what about Bama?" called one of the men, pointing to the young Christian sitting by the open grave.

"We can take care of him later," responded Saley. "The lightning god sounds angry. I don't want to stay out here any longer."

In minutes the men were nowhere in sight of Bama. Just as quickly as the rain had come by the open grave, it stopped. Bama noticed that it was raining very hard between him and the village. The battered Christian stood up and headed towards the nearby forest. He knew that Pastor Mark would protect him if he could reach his village. It meant four days walk through the jungles but he was confident that God would protect him.

The first night Bama fastened himself in the crotch of a tree some fifteen feet above the ground. Just before dark he had found some berries and also a small stream where he enjoyed a good long drink. He took advantage of the cool water to bathe his tired aching body.

As he sat thinking of the events of the day, Bama once again thanked God for sparing his life and for the safety which he now enjoyed.

"Father," he prayed, "thank You for that miracle storm. Thank You, too, for providing the berries and water so I don't have to go to sleep hungry and thirsty."

Bama's head nodded as sleep began to overcome him. "Dear Lord, help me to reach Pastor Mark's village . . . and . . . watch . . . over . . . me . . . as . . . I . . . sleep . . . tonight . . ."

The pitch black jungle night covered the sleeping Christian like a blanket of safety. Bama rested in peace, trusting His God for the days ahead.

(Reprinted by permission of Regular Baptist Press)

7
The
First
Opportunity

The sudden silence of the typewriter caused Lois to look up from where she sat writing her weekly letter to her mother. Bob was pondering over a letter to their supporting churches. The importance of correspondence was not in the spotlight since Bob and Lois Harding had left America on the first leg of their journey to Africa.

"Problem?" asked the young wife, half smiling.

"I don't know what to say about our need for a kerosene refrigerator," answered Bob. "There is no doubt that when we arrive in Africa, we are going to need a refrigerator and . . . refrigerators cost money."

Bob and Lois arrived in Paris seven months before to study the French language. This was a requirement of the mission before they could be cleared for service in the Chad Republic. They left America with the minimum amount of support and found it necessary to budget practically every dollar. As new missionaries, they had very little equipment. They became increasingly aware of the fact that there were some things they could do without, while on the other hand, there were other things which were absolutely necessary.

A kerosene refrigerator was one of those items.

"I think you should put in the letter what we need," spoke Lois, sealing the envelope to her mother. "How else will the people back home know if we don't tell them."

"You're right," responded Bob. "I'll put in the need and we'll trust the Lord to speak to hearts about it."

The next morning, Bob dropped the letter in the mail box. To purchase a new kerosene refrigerator would cost five hundred dollars.

With only enough support to meet their present monthly needs, the couple knew that extra funds had to be supplied from somewhere.

The days passed into weeks while they waited and prayed concerning some kind of leading from the Lord as to what they should do. Then it came, but from a source they never expected. A veteran missionary couple in Chad had to leave the field permanently. The man seriously injured his back when a car he was working on, slipped off the jack and fell on him.

Bob could hardly hold the letter still as he read because of his excitement. "We have to get rid of most of our things and we would like to get everything settled before we leave the field. If you have not made provision for a refrigerator, you will need one when you get here. Our refrigerator is in good condition and we would be happy to sell it to you for $150. There are other items as well that we are listing but we did want to tell you about the refrigerator. Please let us know as soon as possible as there are others who would like to buy it. We want to give you the first opportunity."

"That's the Lord's answer, Lois," said Bob, half shouting. "And it's only $150. Just think, it's already there. That means no shipping or customs charges."

Then Bob's excitement seemed to disappear as fast as it came. "But. . ."

"But what?" asked Lois, reaching out to take her husband's hand.

"But we don't have the money, Honey," answered Bob slowly. "We have only a few dollars balance in our home office account."

"Let's look at it this way, Bob," Lois said in a confident voice, "we have been praying regarding our need for a refrigerator. Out of the heart of Africa comes this unsolicited letter. This has to be the Lord's answer."

"You're right, Lois," answered Bob. "I think we should send our answer right away and tell them that we will buy their refrigerator. We couldn't get a better buy anywhere."

The young couple thanked the Lord for the letter from their coworkers and asked Him to supply the funds so the transfer could be made in the home office from their account to their co-workers' account.

Three days later while Lois was working in the kitchen getting the noon meal ready, she heard Bob's voice out in the hall. "Lois! Here's the answer. We have the answer to our prayers!"

The door flew open and Bob stepped into the tiny apartment kitchen. He held a letter in his hand.

"Listen to this, Honey. It's from Tom Lind. Remember him? He's on the missions committee in that little church in New Jersey."

Bob held the letter before him and began to read. "We received your recent newsletter and saw your need for a kerosene refrigerator. Last night the matter was brought before the church and they voted to give you a gift of $150 toward the purchase of one. We hope that this will be a help to you and that the rest of the funds will come in shortly."

"Just think, Lois, a letter from Africa offering us the first opportunity to buy a refrigerator for the low price of $150 and then, just a few days later, a letter from the church telling us that they are giving us $150."

The young husband stopped a moment and then continued. "I hesitate to think what would have happened had our co-workers not given us the first opportunity to buy it? I'm sure the refrigerator would have sold quickly to someone else."

"True," said Lois, smiling, "but that was impossible, Bob. God answered our prayers by laying it upon their hearts to write and offer us the first opportunity. That refrigerator was saved for us, Honey. God wanted us to have it."

"And to confirm it," responded Bob, "He sent us just the right amount to cover the cost."

Bob and Lois Harding knew in their hearts that the other items mentioned in their newsletter would be supplied as well. Of course, they wanted it to be done in God's way and in His perfect timing.

8
God in Every Detail

(Based on a true incident)

Bob's heart skipped with excitement. Among the pieces of mail was a light blue foreign air-mail envelope. Quickly he pulled the mail from the box and headed for the house.

Ann Miller stood in the doorway waiting for her husband to return with what she hoped would be a letter from Liberia, West Africa.

"We got one from Bill and Jean, Honey," the happy father called.

Anxious to hear what their missionary children had to say, the elderly couple sat down on the front porch steps to read their letter from Africa. Bob quickly opened the envelope and gently pulled out the onion skin paper.

"Dear Mom and Dad," he began reading. "The dry season is really upon us. It hasn't rained for five weeks and we are beginning to see the usual dry season sicknesses at the hospital."

Folded in with the letter was a long list of surgical instruments which Bill asked his father-in-law to send him.

"He doesn't say anything about when or how they should be sent," said Bob. "I'll try to get them this week sometime. Right now the inventory at the store is taking just about every moment of my time."

Bob's good intentions to buy the instruments that week were put aside by the pressures of his store business. The purchase was unintentionally delayed while he cared for his business.

It was two weeks after the receipt of the letter that Bob was abruptly awakened at three in the morning. Bill's letter kept appearing before him. An undescribable feeling overwhelmed him. Not wanting to awaken Ann, he turned over and tried to go back to sleep.

"It's no use," he whispered to himself. "I can't sleep. I've got to get those instruments for Bill tomorrow. I feel like there is an urgent need for them."

Bob shared his burden with Ann in the morning.

"I'm sure the Lord is telling me to get those instruments to Liberia, Honey. For some reason, unknown to us, they must get there as soon as possible."

When he arrived at the store that morning, Bob called a friend who sold surgical equipment.

"Jim, I've got a list here from Bill. I'll send it right over with a driver. Pick out about $200 worth of equipment. I know I can't buy everything he wants so I'll let you choose what you think he would need."

That afternoon, Bob picked up the supply of instruments.

"What would be the fastest way to get them to Liberia, Bill?" he asked his business friend.

Jim thought a moment and then snapped his fingers.

"Why don't you call the ambassador from Liberia, Bob? Maybe he can send the instruments in a diplomatic pouch. After all, it's all for the good of his people."

After some difficulty, Bob finally got through to the Liberian ambassador in Washington.

"I understand, Sir," said the foreign government official, "but if we do it for you, then we will have to do it for all. There are many people who want to send packages to my country."

"But, Mr. Ambassador, these are surgical instruments. They are to be used to help your people," responded Bob.

"I know what you are saying, Mr. Miller, but I just cannot do it." The tone of the ambassador's voice confirmed what he was saying.

"Well, thank you," said the disappointed father.

"Mr. Miller," continued the African diplomat, "have you thought of contacting Republic Steel there in your city? They are sending things all the time to their workers in Liberia. Why don't you try them?"

"Thank you, Sir. Thank you very much. I'll call them immediately."

As soon as he hung up, Bob called Republic Steel. Halfway through his explanation for why he was calling, he was interrupted.

"I'm sorry, Mr. Miller, but we just can't do it for you. If we did it once and the news got out, there would be no end to it."

"Do you have a policy against it?" asked Bob.

"No, we don't have any regulations that say we can't do it," answered the executive at the steel company. "Like I said before, there would probably be no end to it. We'd be taking things for people all the time."

"I know this sounds strange," said Bob, "but I have a feeling deep within me that these surgical instruments are urgently needed. I've got to get them to my son-in-law as soon as possible. Somebody's life might depend on them getting there in time."

The other end of the line was silent. Finally the steel company executive spoke.

"When can you get the instruments to me?"

"Within an hour," responded Bob, his heart beating with excitement. "I'll bring them over myself."

Before an hour had passed, the small box of instruments was in the possession of the steel company and was lined up with the other items destined for Liberia.

"Praise the Lord, Honey," said Bob that evening as he and Ann sat at the dining room table. "The instruments will be on their way tomorrow morning. Bill could have them within a week."

The plane landed at Roberts Field, located forty miles from Monrovia, its capital. The small box of instruments was unloaded along with many other boxes. The steel company official carefully checked his baggage to see that everything was there. He placed his hand on the small box of instruments. For some strange reason, he felt that he should deliver it personally.

"Where is the American hospital?" he asked a policeman at the airport.

"It's on the road to Monrovia, Sir. Your taxi driver will know the place."

The American businessman hailed a taxi and asked the driver to take him to the American hospital. A half hour later, as he got out of the taxi carrying the small box in his arms, the steel company representative had a feeling that what he was doing was pretty important. Upon entering the hospital, he asked for Dr. Hyde.

"He's in surgery now, Sir," said one of the nurses. "He should be out in about thirty minutes."

"I have to go on to the city," answered the visitor, "but I wanted to deliver this package personally. Tell the doctor that if he has any questions he can contact Ed Day at Republic Steel. I'll be returning to the states a week from today."

Bill was thrilled to find the box of instruments when he came out of surgery.

"Dad sure got that here in a hurry," the happy doctor said to his wife, Jean, later at the house. "I haven't checked the list yet to see what he sent, but what I've seen so far looks good."

Two days later, Bill and Jean were awakened at dawn by their five-year-old son, Jimmy.

"Dad! Come! Hurry, Dad!"

The young doctor raced to his son's bed and found Jimmy doubled up with pain. He recognized the trouble immediately. Jimmy was stricken with a strangulated hernia. Bill acted swiftly as he carefully worked to reduce the serious hernia. Within a short time, the missionary doctor saw success.

When they were alone, Bill told Jean that Jimmy needed surgery as soon as possible.

"I'm sending word up to Dr. Henry at the Swedish mission to ask him to do the surgery." A tear trickled down his face. "I don't want to perform the operation on Jimmy unless it is absolutely necessary."

By noon, Dr. Henry arrived for his delicate task. At one o'clock, Jimmy was prepared for surgery. The two doctors prayed together before Dr. Henry took the scalpel.

Bill stood by his medical co-worker throughout the operation. Some of the newly delivered instruments were needed for the surgery.

"These are beautiful instruments, Bill," said the visiting surgeon as he tied the last suture. "Without them, I'm afraid I would have had a difficult time."

The next few days saw remarkable improvement in Jimmy. It was the third day after the operation that Bill sat writing to Jean's parents.

"Thank you, Dad, for sending the instruments when you did. I know you had no idea that some of the ones you chose on the list were just the ones needed for Jimmy's operation. Isn't it comforting to know that we serve a God who loves and cares for us in every detail—even in the most minute details?"

Bill stopped writing and laid down his pen. He bowed his head to once again thank God for sparing Jimmy's life.

(Reprinted by permission of Regular Baptist Press)

9
My
Heart
Sings

Big Bear placed the last piece of firewood on top of the six foot pile.

"That should keep me until the thaw begins," he grunted to himself, kicking angrily at a piece of wood projecting from the stack. The husky Blackfoot Indian lived alone in a small cottage in the hills of Montana. For years he went through the same routine in preparing for the cold winter months. As he walked to his one-room log cabin, he cast a glance down the snow-covered path which led off into the distant valley.

"I hope I never see him again!" said Big Bear to himself. He was thinking of his last visitor, Missionary Bill Price, just the week before. In the little settlement where the missionaries lived, everyone had heard about the wicked old Indian who lived up the valley in the hills. The name of Big Bear struck fear in many hearts.

Emily Price looked out the frosted kitchen window to see her husband just coming in through the front gate. She hurried to open the door for him.

"These groceries sure get heavy," laughed Bill, putting the two bags down on the kitchen table. "They're talking about a big snow coming in this evening."

Emily began putting the groceries away.

"This may sound strange, Bill, but for some reason I've been thinking a lot about Big Bear today. Some of the ladies in my Bible class were talking about him this morning."

"Well, I can testify to the fact that he is not a very pleasant man," responded Bill. "I don't believe I'll ever forget that shot he fired over my head last week when I tried to approach his cabin."

"But it was only a warning shot, Bill," added Emily through a broad grin.

"Warning or not, that man is dangerous and from what I hear about him, anyone approaching his log cabin is laying his life on the line."

That night the snow began to fall as was predicted. By morning, ten inches of the white fluff covered the ground. Bill arose early to shovel off the front walk.

"They don't know if he's alive or dead." Bill looked up to see where the voice was coming from. Coming down the snow-covered street was the town mayor and his assistant.

"Good morning, Mayor Jones," called Bill, waving to the town official. "Did something happen during the night?"

The two men walked over to where Bill stood, leaning on his shovel.

"It's Big Bear," replied the mayor. "Someone spotted a fire in the hills early this morning and a skier has just returned with the news that Big Bear's log cabin burned to the ground. There was no trace of him, but, of course, it's too early to tell if anything happened to him."

The three men discussed the new developments for several minutes and then separated. Bill returned to the house to share the news.

"I'm going up there, Honey. I just tuned up the snowmobile yesterday and this would be a good trip to try it out."

The snowmobile skimmed over the snow with each minute bringing Bill closer to the destroyed cabin site. Reaching the path leading up through the trees, Bill maneuvered the machine with the greatest of skill.

"Father," he whispered, "help me find Big Bear alive. He needs You, Lord. Help me, I pray, to find him."

Bill was thankful that the snow had stopped falling. Reaching the site of the fire, he quickly searched the ruins. Now and then a burst of flame would break out among the timbers. After fifteen minutes, Bill decided that Big Bear had escaped the fire and was no doubt in the nearby forest. He climbed into his snowmobile and began a large circle around the burned dwelling in search of tracks.

Just as he was about to complete the circle, Bill noticed the half-filled tracks leading off into the pines. He went as far as he could with the snowmobile and then continued on by foot.

"Big Bear!" called the missionary. "Big Bear! It's the missionary, Bill Price. I've come to help you. Do you hear me?"

Other than his own echo, silence greeted Bill's call.

About an hour into the forest, Bill spotted a small column of smoke coming up through the trees below him. Quickly, but quietly, he made his way down the side of the mountain. Finally through the trees Bill saw where the smoke was coming from. There was a small cave with an opening no more than three feet high. In minutes, he was standing outside.

"Ohhhhhh . . . ."

Bill's heart jumped when he heard the groan.

"Big Bear!" called Bill. "It's the missionary, Bill Price."

"Help me," came the reply. Bill scrambled into the darkened cave. He waited a moment for his eyes to adjust to the darkness. There, curled up alongside the fire, was Big Bear. His clothes were badly burned, exposing an arm, part of his back and a leg. Bill knew that Big Bear needed immediate medical attention.

"Dear Father," prayed Bill so Big Bear could hear him, "please help Big Bear. Father, spare his life and help me to know what to do."

Bill took off his quilted jacket and spread it over the suffering Indian. He hurried outside and in the nearest clearing gathered wood and made a fire. It was difficult working in the fresh snow. In ten minutes, Bill had a fire going, sending a column of smoke high into the sky. He checked on Big Bear again, added wood to the fire in the cave and headed back to the snowmobile.

"Send somebody to help me, Dear Father," prayed Bill as he hurried back through the forest. He made good time and within forty-five minutes he broke out of the pines into the opening.

"Thank you, Lord," he prayed out loud as he saw two snowmobiles beside the ruins. Four young men had come from the village to investigate the fire and even though they had heard many stories about Big Bear, they were glad to hear he was alive.

Within minutes the five men, carrying food, coffee and a box of medical supplies which Bill had in his snowmobile, entered the pines and headed at a rapid pace for the cave. Bill was thankful for the fire which he had built because the column of smoke allowed the men to take a shortcut to reach the cave.

"I'm back, Big Bear," called Bill, stooping down to crawl into the cave.

Being careful to protect the burned areas of Big Bear's body, a blanket was wrapped around him and he was placed on a crude stretcher made of several poles and a blanket. The five men slowly made their way back to the snowmobiles with their precious cargo.

The men who helped Bill were just beginning their career as lumberjacks. They had heard of Prices' ministry but had never attended any of the services. The turn of events involving Big Bear caused the men to think of their own spiritual needs. As they walked along, Bill had the opportunity to tell them about Christ and what He did for them.

"I know that story," whispered Big Bear. "An old Indian woman told me about Jesus one day when I was a little boy, but that's the only time I heard anything about Him."

"I was coming to tell you that story last week, Big Bear, when you shot at me," said Bill, looking into the Indian's face.

"You can tell it to me now, White Man. I'm not going anywhere and I have a lot of time to listen."

Bill was just finishing the salvation story as the men entered the clearing.

"My heart has never sung, White Man," said Big Bear. "I have no god to love me and watch over me as you have."

"You can have Jesus right now, Big Bear, if you accept Him. He is waiting to forgive you of your sins and to give you everlasting life."

"I'm so wicked, White Man, but you say He can wipe out all that wickedness?"

"Yes, He can, Big Bear," responded Bill. With Bill's help, Big Bear prayed, confessing his sins and asking Christ to save him. The moment he finished praying he looked up into the five faces. A smile spread across his face.

"My heart sings, White Man. My heart sings."

Tears came to Bill's eyes as he glanced from Big Bear into the faces of the four lumberjacks.

"Sir, I want my heart to sing, too," said one of the men as he shook Bill's hand.

Again heads were bowed as a new born babe entered God's family. There was no response from the other three men, but Bill knew their hearts were deeply touched.

Radio contact was made from the village and within two hours a helicopter airlifted Big Bear to a city hospital forty miles away. Unknown to Bill and Emily Price, within five weeks Big Bear, the converted Indian whose heart now sang, would be back, but this time living in the village and becoming a vital part of their local church ministry.

(Reprinted by permission of Regular Baptist Press)

10
Struck
by
Lightning

The rumble of thunder in the distance prompted Sherm to look up from underneath the open hood of the pickup truck. Far off in the East he spotted some dark clouds.

"Well, it looks like the beginning of our rainy season, Koutou," spoke the first-term missionary to his African helper. Sherm stretched to help ease the kink in his back.

"The first rains are late this year, Mr. McElroy," responded Koutou. "When they come from the East it always means a bad storm."

"Those clouds must be at least ten miles away," mumbled Sherm more to himself than to his friend. He quickly put the air filter back on top of the carburetor and fastened it in place. Sherm and his wife, Diane had only been in Africa for two years, but they really loved the people and wanted to gain their confidence. Lately, however, they had sensed disinterest on the part of many of the nearby village people. Sherm was thankful for Koutou and his faithfulness.

"Let's go, Koutou. I want to clean the carburetor on the light plant before the storm reaches us. Last night the light plant sputtered several times. I think there must be some dirt in the fuel line."

Except for the small gathering of clouds in the distance, everything looked like an ordinary dry season day. The heat from the mid-day sun seemed even a bit hotter than usual. The two men walked swiftly to the rear of the open carpenter shop where the small gasoline engine generator was bolted to a concrete base.

Sherm quickly and expertly disassembled the small carburetor. Now and then he would glance at the approaching storm.

"It's still a long way off, Mr. McElroy," said the African worker, pointing to the distant clouds. The anxious missionary looked at his watch. He had been working on the light plant for ten minutes.

"I found the problem, Koutou," Sherm said, turning to his friend.

"You have plenty of time to get it back together. The rumbles are getting louder and longer, but the clouds don't seem to be coming very fast." Koutou was watching the sky.

Just then an ear-splitting crash shook the ground. Flames leaped from the gasoline engine. Sherm was thrown on his back to the brick floor and there laid stunned and helpless.

"Throw sand on it, Koutou! Throw sand on the fire!" Sherm called.

Koutou acted quickly, grabbing up handfuls of sand and throwing them onto the flaming engine. Just then, Sherm heard Diane cry for help from the house. The frightened missionary tried to get up but fell back on the floor. He had no feeling on the right side of his body.

"Help me, Koutou," he called to his friend who had successfully put out the fire. "Help me get to Mrs. McElroy and the children."

Once on his feet, Sherm found he could hop on his left leg. Koutou walked alongside, assisting him.

To Sherm's relief, Diane appeared on the back veranda. She was holding the right side of her head and with her left hand she held tightly to little Penny's hand.

"Are you all right, Diane?" called Sherm as Koutou helped him up on the veranda. "Are Penny and Danny O.K.?"

"My head hurts," answered Diane, her pale face distorted with pain. "Penny and I were thrown to the floor when the lightning hit. She was washing her hands at the bathroom sink and I had just walked away from Danny's crib. He's all right. He didn't even wake up with that terrible noise."

Just then Ruth Barry, the station nurse, came running around the corner of the house. "Sherm! Diane! Is everyone all right?"

A quick examination found no serious casualties. The feeling in Sherm's right side was beginning to return.

"I was out in my garden when I heard this terrible crash," spoke Ruth. "I saw the storm in the distance, but it was so far away I never gave it a second thought."

"That's what I thought," added Sherm, rubbing his arm and leg.

"The bolt of lightning struck the tree right alongside my house. It not only split the tree, but it made a big crack on the side wall," continued the nurse.

"That's how it got into the wiring and made its way to the light plant," said Sherm. "The electric wires run along on top of the wall at that place."

"Look at that," called Diane, pointing to the wall of their house. "The fuse box is gone!" Scattered around the veranda were pieces of the metal box. "And the light bulbs are gone, too," added Diane, pointing to the light sockets overhead.

Ruth slowly shook her head in amazement. "Praise the Lord we're all safe. Look what the lightning did to that metal box and here we are with no cuts or broken bones. That's a miracle!"

Koutou, who had been listing to the conversation, raised his hand to get their attention. "I would like to say something, my friends. What has happened today is a testimony of the power of God. Bamara the witchdoctor has made it known among the villagers that he plans to bring death to you missionaries. No one has wanted to say anything about it but many of the people out in the villages have been waiting to see what would happen. Today, Mr. McElroy, our God has answered. I know the lightning hurt you and Mrs. McElroy and little Penny, but thank the Lord your lives have been spared."

"And two things more," continued Koutou. "What has happened today will really weaken Bamara's hold on our people. He won't be happy to hear about this. I know, too, that the church will be filled on Sunday to see our miracle missionaries. Even the fire from the skies couldn't destroy you with God's protection upon you."

Koutou put his hand on Sherm's shoulder. "And Mr. McElroy, I want to travel with you everywhere you go among our people. You see, I'm a witness to what has happened and I have some good words to say about it, especially to Bamara."

Sherm smiled as he reached out to shake Koutou's hand. "We'll tell the story together, Koutou—the story of how God spoke through the lightning."

(Reprinted by permission of Regular Baptist Press)

11

The God That Lost Its Head

(A true story)

"**H**ow much farther is the village, Andrew?"

Bob Cousins squinted his eyes as he looked into the setting sun. The bright orange glare along with the spatters of mud on the windshield made it nearly impossible to see the road.

"It's around the next bend, Mr. Cousins," answered the African Christian. "If Keke is there, our stay may be very short. That's if we get into the village at all."

Nearly all the people in the tiny African country knew about Keke, the fearful witchdoctor. Stories of his powerful witchcraft activities traveled the African grapevine for hundreds of miles. He was one of the most feared in that part of Africa.

Word among the Christian population was that the Gospel had never been preached in the village of Koui. Keke's father as well as his grandfather were witchdoctors. They saw to it that the village of Koui was kept for the worship of Satan. Only once did a missionary try to enter the village to preach the Gospel and he barely escaped with his life. Eye witnesses reported that a poison arrow missed him by inches.

"How did the village get the name of Koui, Andrew?" questioned the inquisitive missionary. "That means physical death in my language."

"You see, Mr. Cousins, if any of our tribe's people associate themselves in any way with death, that means they live close to Satan and are given a special portion of his power. In fact, all my people believe that the village of Koui has Satan's protecting hand upon it. When you see the village god, you will understand what I am saying."

The tan pickup truck came around the bend and there stretched out for two hundred yards was the much talked about village.

"What's that tall thing in the center of the village?" asked Bob as he slowed the approach of the truck.

"That's the village god," responded Andrew. "It is very sacred to the villagers. It's actually a giant drum. A buffalo skin is stretched across the hollow top. Every full moon, a man appointed by the witchdoctor climbs to the top and beats the drum for about an hour."

Bob had more questions about the strange looking drum but they had reached the village and an unfriendly looking crowd was rapidly approaching them.

"Why do you stop in my village, missionary?" called a tall ugly looking man. Bob's questioner had several brass rings on each ear. A leopard skin was wrapped about him.

"He knows who you are," whispered Andrew. "The grapevine has announced our coming."

Once again, Bob realized the ingenuity of the world's primitive peoples. Certainly, their intelligence could not be determined by standards of the so called civilized world. He had often said that every culture has its own geniuses.

"Hello, Keke," spoke Bob with the voice of confidence. "I've come to visit with you and your people. If you will permit us, we would like to spend the night here in your village."

"We don't need your presence, white man. You and your African traitors can get back into that truck and keep going. We don't want you here. Now go!"

"But, we don't dislike you. We've come to share with you some good news," continued Bob.

"I know what your good news is all about," said the witchdoctor. "It's about Jesus and we don't want Him here in this village."

Keke pointed towards the 30 foot drum. "There's our god. It speaks forth with thunder. Those blood stains covering it shows our devotion. We don't need your God. He is a stranger to us."

Bob looked at the tall hollow log. Pegs were stuck in holes from top to bottom to allow the drummer to climb it. He could not help but notice the dried blood stains which covered nearly every bit of its surface.

The witchdoctor stepped toward Bob. "White man, your blood will be the next given to our god unless you leave now. I'm about to send one of my men to the top to thunder out the good news of our latest sacrifice."

"We're leaving," spoke up Andrew. "My white man doesn't fully understand your ways, Keke."

Within seconds, the men were back in the truck and returning back down the road. "But why not continue on further?" Bob asked.

"They may block the road on our return, Mr. Cousins," answered one of the men. "It is best that we go this way. Please trust our judgement."

That night the men stopped in a small village where the chief turned over his hut to the visitors. He summoned several women to cook a meal of chicken and manioc. As usual, strong coffee was served with the heavily spiced food. After the meal, the chief called the villagers together to hear Bob and his African companions give their testimonies. At the invitation, four adults and two children indicated they wanted to receive Christ as their Savior.

Later that night as the men rested on grass mats scattered about the floor of the large hut, they spoke of the day's events.

"God will open the village of Koui some day, Mr. Cousins," said one of the men.

"I'm sure He will," agreed Bob. "Let's all of us pray every day that that wonderful day will come soon. I'm trusting that when it does happen, we will enter the village by invitation from Keke and that he will ask us to preach the Gospel to the entire village."

Upon their return to the mission station, the story was told over and over again how Keke threatened the life of their missionary. Not only did the people pray together as families for Koui to be opened to the Gospel but they also prayed publicly in the church services.

It was sixteen months later when the answer came. Bob had just crawled out from underneath the truck. He had punctured the gas tank with a flying rock and had to take it off to repair it. He heard the squeal of a bicycle's brakes and looked up to see a stranger get off his bicycle and start towards him.

"Hello, Mr. Cousins. I've come with a message for you from Keke. He's sick and can't seem to get better."

Bob greeted the stranger with a handshake and quickly opened the soiled envelope.

"Mr. Cousins, I ask you to come and help me. I have a sickness working me and no one seems to be able to help me; not even our village god. I need your medicine and help from your God. I have many words inside of me to tell you when you come. Signed Keke."

Bob's heart leaped within him. He asked one of his workmen to take the stranger to Andrew's house and to tell Andrew to be ready to travel immediately. He then ran into the house to tell Betty the good news.

"Betty!" he called as he entered the house. "I've good news, Honey. I'm going to Koui today."

The pretty brunette wife emerged from the kitchen with a questioned look on her face. "You're going to do what?"

"I've just received a note from witchdoctor Keke. He's sick and he wants me to come and help him. I may have to bring him back to the dispensary."

Bob read the note to Betty who was already busy getting the food box ready for the trip. "I'll tell Andrew and maybe one or two other men. If we leave now, I'm sure we can be there before dark."

Even though the road was in terrible condition from the heavy rains, the men made good time. They arrived at Koui with about an hour of daylight left. To their surprise, Keke was sitting outside his hut in a chaise lounge. Because of his weakened condition he stayed seated as his visitors approached.

"Hello, Mr. Cousins. My heart is glad that you came so soon."

"Hello, Keke," responded Bob who shook the witchdoctor's hand. "I came as soon as I received your note. Thank you for asking me to come."

"Sit down, Mr. Cousins. I want to tell you something very important."

Keke then pointed to the giant drum out in the center of the village. It was perfectly silhouetted in the light of the setting sun. The termites had eaten at its base causing it to lean sharply to one side. The buffalo skin that once covered the top was now rotted with parts of it hanging over the sides of the decayed log.

"That is no longer my god, Mr. Cousins. The termites have eaten its feet and the sun and rain have destroyed its head. Its thundering voice is gone and so is its power. Our god is dead."

"You mean your god has lost its head, Keke?" asked Bob in a serious tone of voice.

"Its head and its heart," responded the witchdoctor. For ten moons, I asked it to help me but I see now that it was helpless. I am getting worse by the day. Mr. Cousins, I believe your God can help me and if He does, my village will belong to Him."

Through watching Betty in her dispensary work, Bob was familiar with many diseases. A quick examination of Keke revealed the possibility of several things wrong with him. While looking over the witchdoctor, the missionary explained to him how God does work many times through people as well as medicines. He told Keke that the best place for him would be to go and stay at the dispensary for a while.

"You and your men can stay in my hut with me. But before we go to our beds tonight, I want you to tell my people about Jesus."

Bob and the three Africans gave their testimonies, each telling what Christ had done for them. Andrew then asked how many of the villagers wanted to receive Jesus as their Savior. Six adults voiced their desire to become Christians. The witchdoctor and his visitors talked long into the night about the Gospel.

"I know you men are tired," spoke Keke, "but I just can't get enough of your good words about God. I've been doing some thinking. Why should I wait to see if I'm going to get better before I accept Jesus into my heart? From what my ears are hearing, its my heart that is really sick and it can be made well right now."

"You are right, Keke," said Andrew. "God wants to make your heart well tonight—right here in your hut."

The men gathered around the sick witchdoctor as he confessed his sins and asked Jesus to become his Savior. The moment he finished praying, he looked up at the men. His eyes twinkled in the light of the kerosene lamp.

"Your God is my God, now," he beamed. "Tomorrow, before we leave, you all can finish the job on the drum. I want to see it destroyed before I go. After all," he said with a grin, "what good is a god that can't stand up and has lost its head."

The four men laughed at Keke's remarks. Andrew then led the group in prayer and a short time later, they were sound asleep. A peaceful look was on Bob's face as he slept. Keke was saved, Koui would soon have a new name and the village was already open to the Gospel.

(Reprinted by permission of Regular Baptist Press)

12

God
Was
in the
Wind

(Based on a True Story)

The shrill of the hurricane winds sent chills up Carol's backbone. The young missionary wife, alone in the small cottage, sat crouched on the floor of the tiny closet. Her hands tightly gripped the flashlight which provided some assurance for her in the total darkness of the room. As she listened to the roar of the raging ocean just a quarter of a mile away, she visioned the devastating effects it was likely having that very moment on the populated area along the shore.

"Dear Lord," prayed Carol, "please help those dear people and watch over Brinson wherever he is."

Thoughts of her husband at the construction site of the new medical work caused the young wife to cringe. Because of its higher elevation on the southern coast of Haiti, the newly purchased land some three miles away was an open target for the 150 mile winds. She knew that Brinson and his national helper, Ely, faced the full fury of the hurricane as it swept across the tiny Caribbean nation. The young missionary's heart skipped a beat when a large palm tree dropped with a loud crash alongside the small house.

"Father," she breathed, "protect all of us in this storm."

A quick glance at her watch told her it was 2:30 a.m. She stood up with a start, hearing terrible crashing sounds above her. Gingerly Carol moved out into a larger room and made her way up the steps. The wind and rain beat heavy on her. Halfway up Carol noticed the wind had taken off nearly all the roof, leaving very little of the metal sheeting and wood structure behind. Quickly she retreated to the safety of the room below and returned to the closet.

"Surely," she whispered to herself," this house can't stand much more."

Carol sat listening to the roar of the ocean. It seemed like any moment the cottage would be blown apart. Sleep was impossible for her.

About an hour later Carol was again brought to her feet with a loud bang. She again left the safety of the small closet to investigate what had happened. The wind had forced the door open, tearing out the screws holding the bolts. Mustering all her strength, she pulled some furniture toward the door. Forcing it closed, she placed the furniture behind it. Within minutes the heavy door burst open again, throwing the furniture about the room. Carol made her way to the door to try and close it.

Reaching the door, Carol gasped when she saw the dark form. There, standing beside the doorway, held tight against the wall by the force of the wind, was a young boy. She quickly grabbed the young lad and pulled him inside. Together they retreated to the safety of the closet.

"Who are you? What are you doing out in a storm like this?" called Carol above the noise of the hurricane.

"I've been afraid to go home, Madame," answered the wide-eyed boy.

Carol noticed he was shaking, probably from fear as well as from the cold. She stepped out into the larger room and quickly returned with a blanket and put it around the boy. His teeth chattered as he spoke.

"I was on my way home right after it became dark, but the winds were so strong I went into a house down by the sea. Before we realized what had happened, the house blew apart. We all scattered in different directions, looking for shelter. I made my way up the road until I came to your house. When I saw the door open, I headed for it and then I saw you inside.

Carol turned on the flashlight every now and then to see if her visitor was all right.

"What is your name?" Carol asked.

"Andrew," came the immediate reply.

"Well, Andrew, it looks like you and I are going to be here for the rest of the night and since we are, I would like to talk to you about something that is very important."

Andrew listened to the American missionary as she explained to him how God loved him, but because of his sin, the judgment of death was upon him. She then went on to tell him how Christ willingly paid the penalty for his sin and that forgiveness was his if he would only accept God's Son by faith.

The young lad listened intently but showed no response to the Gospel message.

"Those are good words, Madame," said Andrew, "but I don't believe my heart is ready to accept Jesus."

The time passed quickly and soon the gray light of dawn could be seen coming through the top of the roofless building. By daylight the storm was passed and Andrew decided it was time to continue on home. Carol's heart was heavy as the young Haitian teenager bid farewell to her. She knew he was leaving without Christ as his Savior. Tears filled her eyes as she saw him disappear down the road. Moments later Brinson appeared on foot with Ely.

"I couldn't get through by road, Honey," said the tired husband. "Trees are down all over the place and there must be hundreds of homes destroyed."

A quick survey of the cottage showed extensive damage.

"Praise the Lord you are safe," said Brinson, putting his arms around Carol. "I just can't imagine what it must have been like while you were here and especially before Andrew came. We must look him up and keep in contact with him."

During the next week, between repairs on their home, Brinson and Carol successfully found Andrew. His parents' home had been destroyed but his family had survived the hurricane.

"In two weeks Mrs. McGowan and I are returning to Port-au-Prince, Andrew. You say you have never been to the capital city. Why not accept our invitation and come visit us for a week? We'll provide the transportation for you."

Andrew was delighted to hear such an invitation from his new friends.

"I accept your invitation," he said, smiling. "I have always wanted to see the big city."

Brinson could only purchase most of his building supplies in Port-au-Prince. The little seaside town where they were temporarily located until they moved to the medical site had very little construction materials in the stores. Andrew was a very happy Haitian boy as he climbed into the missionaries' Landrover for the trip to the capital.

The first sight of Port-au-Prince brought a cry from Andrew's lips.

"I see it," he called, pointing to the city in the distance. "Look at all those houses."

Brinson and Carol smiled at each other. Within fifteen minutes they were entangled in the busy, honking, overcrowded traffic of the country's largest city. Andrew never dreamed there were so many cars and trucks. He was all eyes as he looked from side to side, trying to take it all in.

Upon arriving home, Brinson and Carol were greeted by shouts of welcome from their neighbors who were happy to see that they had survived the storm. Within an hour their fellow missionaries arrived from other parts of the city. Andrew was thrilled in the way each one accepted him. It seemed like they had always known him.

"We are going to go to prayer meeting tonight at one of our co-worker's homes," said Brinson to Andrew two days after their arrival in Port-au-Prince. "They are inviting us over for dinner along with the other missionaries and then we will stay for our midweek prayer meeting. We always invite our Haitian neighbors to meet with us, too."

Andrew was not too surprised to hear about the prayer meeting. He noticed his missionary friends talked to their God many times. It seemed they had a special relationship with Him as they even thanked Him for the food they ate. The longer Andrew was with them the more he realized they had something he did not possess. Never before had he seen such love for others as there was among the missionaries. Andrew was brought into their conversations just as if he had always been with them.

After the meal the missionaries gathered in the front room along with a number of Haitians who came for the meeting. Veteran missionary, Don Block, led the group in singing several hymns and then opened the Bible for the evening message. Again, Andrew drank in every word. At the close of the message, Don asked everyone to bow their heads.

"God loves you," he said, "and His Son, Jesus, died for you. If you will call upon Him, He will forgive you of your sins and give you eternal life."

The missionary's words struck hard upon Andrew's heart. At the invitation to accept Christ, the young Haitian stood to his feet. Brinson took his new friend aside to talk and pray with him. It was a blessed time as the missionaries and Andrew talked together after the service. They all listened as he recounted the night he fled to the cottage for refuge.

"I thought I was going to die in the storm, but God was in the wind. He blew me right to the open door where Madame found me and brought me in."

Carol squeezed Brinson's hand and whispered to her husband.

"God really was in the wind, Honey. He used it to bring Andrew to us and to Himself."

(Reprinted by permission of Regular Baptist Press)

13

Ten
Long
Years

(A true story)

"Look, Dad, I'm not going to church. Now, that's all there is to it. I've had enough of church for awhile. You and Mom go on without me. I'll see you when you come home!"

Wayne threw his coat into a nearby chair and headed for his room. Never before had he spoken like that to his parents. Roy and Joyce Yates were numb as they watched their only son disappear down the hall.

"Wayne!" called the shocked father. The bedroom door closed, cutting off any further communication.

Tearfully, the unhappy mother looked at her husband. "What's happened to Wayne, Roy? He hasn't seemed like the same boy we left since we arrived home."

The bewildered look on her husband's face answered her question.

"I don't know, Honey. I really don't know what has happened to him."

Roy and Joyce Yates had gone to Chad, Africa, right after they had graduated from Bible school. It was during their first term of service there that Wayne was born. The young American loved the country of his birth. He learned the tribal languages as quickly as he learned English. He played and grew up with the African children.

When he was nine years old, Wayne accepted Christ as his Savior. It happened one Sunday morning after his father had finished preaching. Young Wayne got up from his seat and walked to the front of the tiny dried mud block grass-roofed church building.

"I want to get saved, Dad," said the weeping boy. "I've just been fooling you and mom. I'm really not saved."

Roy Yates took his son aside that Sunday morning and had the joy of leading him to Christ.

Wayne went back to Africa only one more time after that term. Because there was no provision for a high school education on the field other than by correspondence, his parents thought it best for him to remain with his aunt and uncle. They had children about his age and it was felt that Wayne would adjust better to the separation if he was with family.

The departure of Roy and Joyce was a heartbreaking experience for the young man.

"Just think, Wayne," said his mother as she hugged him at the airport, "we can look forward to your graduation from high school. It's only four years away. Dad and I will be counting the days."

The teenage lad choked back the tears. If only he could share his grief with his parents but he was sure they wouldn't understand. Wayne watched the plane until it disappeared into the low-hanging clouds. Turning his head, he began making his way down the long corridor to the parking lot. He didn't want his aunt and uncle to see him cry.

"Why did you leave me?" sobbed Wayne once he was back in his room. "Why did you have to go back again?" The hot tears burst forth like a flood coursing down his face. Never had he cried so hard in his life. The lump in his throat made it difficult for him to breathe. Even though his parents had tried to prepare him for this difficult time of separation, he knew he wasn't ready for it.

Life was especially trying for Wayne the first few weeks. His aunt way possible to compensate for the void they left in his life. His cousins did what they could to help him, but the separation was like a very bitter pill for the homesick lad. Many nights he cried himself to sleep.

"God, why did You do this to me?" he repeatedly asked. "What have I done to You to deserve this?"

In his personal life, Wayne was rapidly growing bitter toward the Lord. Outwardly, it appeared that he was getting over the pain of separation. The battle raged within him until finally one Sunday morning it surfaced.

"I'm not going to church, Aunt Vera. I don't feel well."

When he had another excuse the following Sunday, his aunt and uncle began to have suspicions that something more serious was wrong.

"But why don't you want to go to church, Wayne?" asked his Uncle Don one morning. "Your mom and dad would be hurt if they knew about this."

To keep peace in the family, the frustrated boy started attending church again. He figured that the more of his activities he kept to himself, the better it would be for everyone. The next three years were difficult years for the young man. Every now and then a problem would show up between him and his aunt and uncle, but for the most part, he was able to keep his private affairs hidden from the family. Even his cousins thought things were going along all right for Wayne.

"The Lord willing we plan to arrive on May 5th at Chicago." The letter from his parents gave Wayne the flight number and time of their arrival. Knowing the change that had taken place in his own life, the high school senior wondered how he would tell his mother and father that he no longer loved God or wanted to have anything to do with Him. He had attended church regularly so no one could accuse him of that. Likewise, he was careful to do his smoking and drinking away from any of the church and family contacts. Wayne, very cleverly, had lived a double life without raising any suspicions against him.

It was an exciting time for Roy and Joyce Yates as they arrived in Chicago. Even Wayne showed his emotions when his father hugged him. Since he had missed church only a few times in the past four years, his aunt and uncle had not said anything to his parents.

Three weeks had gone by since their arrival from Africa when Wayne decided to let them know of his feelings against the Lord.

"Wayne," called his father softly outside the bedroom door. "Can I come in and talk with you?"

"OK, come on in but I know you won't like what I have to say," answered the young man.

Roy and Joyce Yates didn't want to believe what their son was saying to them.

"I just don't have any feelings toward God," said Wayne. "He's only given me a rough time the past four years. As soon as I can, I'll find an apartment and move out. That way, you won't see the rotten things I'm doing."

The next two weeks were filled with heartaches and worry for the burdened parents. Wayne had informed them that he would be moving in with some friends at the first of the month. It seemed every waking moment was spent by Roy and Joyce thinking of their son. The first of the month, Wayne moved out. Several rough-looking young men appeared at the Yates home to help him move his things.

The weeping mother thought her heart would break as she hugged her son. Grief was written all over her husband's face. His lips trembled when he tried to say good-bye but no words came forth. He was certain that spiritual tragedy was in store for their beloved son.

The days became months and the months, years. Now and then, Wayne phoned his parents but eventually, the calls stopped. Wayne Yates had slipped out of his parents' lives.

The heartbroken parents prayed faithfully for their son. It was not unusual for Joyce to awaken during the night to hear her husband praying for Wayne.

"Father," prayed Roy one morning, "it's been ten years now since our Wayne has left us. You know all about him, Lord. We've asked You many times to bring him back into fellowship with Yourself. Dear Father, please bring our Wayne back to us soon."

It was a week later on Saturday night when the call came. Joyce was reading the evening paper and Roy had just finished studying his Sunday school lesson. The aged-looking man picked up the phone.

"Hello," he said in a tired voice.

"Hi, Dad. How are you and Mom?"

The surprised father was at a loss for words. "We're fine, Son. How are you doing?"

"I'm OK, Dad. I'm calling to tell you and Mom that I'll be coming home tonight."

Wayne's voice broke. "Everything is all right now, Dad. I've squared things with the Lord but I'll tell you and Mom about it when I get home. I want to be there to go to church with you tomorrow."

Joyce saw the look on her husband's face and knew it was good news.

"Thank the Lord, Son," answered the happy father wiping his eyes.

"Wayne has come back to the Lord, Honey. He's coming home tonight."

It was near midnight when Wayne arrived. The thrilled parents were on the porch to meet him. Tears flowed freely as the three of them sat and talked.

"I opened a can of beer and turned on the TV to watch a movie. I reached for my cigarettes and when I saw the package was empty, I rolled it up and threw it across the room. I saw it hit my Bible which was on a shelf under the TV."

"Your Bible?" exclaimed his mother.

"Yes, Mom," answered Wayne. "It was the one you and Dad gave to me for my graduation. I never had the heart to throw it away or misuse it. I always kept it somewhere. I've not been ashamed of you. It was the Lord I wanted to hurt." Wayne paused and then continued.

"The cigarette package hit the Bible and bounced away. Dad, it was just like I had hit the Lord. Something happened inside me. I immediately saw my sin and my terrible situation. I got down on my knees right there and confessed everything I could think of—everything."

Wayne reached out and took his mother's hand.

"Mom and Dad, I ask your forgiveness, too. I've hurt you both so very much. I know I'll never be able to make it up to you."

"You've made it up tonight, Son," said the joyful father. "Mom and I have prayed for you many times every day since you left. Tonight God has answered our prayers. He has brought you back to Himself just as we knew He would do some day."

A smile spread across Roy's face as he looked at his wife.

"Honey, let's pray with our son. We've waited for this moment for ten long years. Now we'll thank our wonderful God for His answer."

(Reprinted by permission of Regular Baptist Press)

14

Good
News
From
Ngende

The teenaged boy carried on a constant conversation with the man behind him. Between them was a four foot pole which each of them held in their right hand. Ngende was on his way to prayer meeting. The tall Mandja tribesman was one of the most faithful members of the church at Kaga Bandoro. Only once did he miss a regular church service in the past eight years and that was due to a bout with malaria that had him delirious for two days.

"Look, Mommy," cried little Sandy Williams. "Here comes the blind man with the little boy." The missionary child had grown accustomed to seeing Ngende arrive at church with his faithful escort. The seven mile walk from Ngende's village made it necessary for him to start out very early on Sunday morning in order to be in time for Sunday School.

"Shh. Yes, I see him, Honey," whispered the young mother, placing her hand on her little daughter's shoulder.

Pastor Gilbert announced the opening hymn. The congregation began to sing as Ngende entered the church. Halfway down the aisle, he stopped, felt with his toe until he touched the concrete bench. As he pushed in, the people made a place for him though the bench was already crowded. Ngende reached into his pocket and took out a soiled cloth and carefully spread it over the place where he would be sitting. The little boy slid in beside his blind friend. Nan smiled as she watched the two latecomers prove the African thinking that there is always room for one more.

The young missionary wife thought of the testimony that Ngende had shared with Jim and her just the week before. She recalled how the blind man waited for them to come out of their house after he had clapped his hands to let them know that he was there. Jim was the first to speak to Ngende that day.

"Hello, Ngende, how are you? And what brings you to see us?"

The toothless African smiled broadly. "There are two things, Mr. Williams, that bring me to your house. The first thing is that I'm hungry and the second thing is about a meeting we had in my village."

Nan, who had already shaken Ngende's hand, disappeared into the house even before the tall Mandja mentioned his hunger. Ngende knew that whenever he was hungry he could always find food at the missionaries' house.

While Ngende talked, Nan hastily prepared two huge plates of food. What the young boy with Ngende didn't eat, she knew Ngende would. She soon reappeared and Ngende stopped long enough in his conversation with Jim to thank the Lord for the food.

"I realize that you are very busy, my friends," spoke the blind man, "so if you don't mind, I will tell you what happened as I eat."

Jim watched Ngende as he expertly maneuvered the large serving spoon from the plate to his mouth. During the course of the many meals he had eaten at the missionaries' house, they taught him how to use a fork, knife and spoon. Ngende finally settled with a serving spoon.

"It happened so fast I could not believe it," began Ngende, feeling for the mashed potatoes on his plate. Ngende had awakened one night and knew that it still must be dark because the roosters had not yet begun to crow. The stillness in the village told him the people were asleep. Then he heard it. Someone was in his house. He smelled a lantern which meant they were using it in order to see.

"Who is it?" he called. No one answered. He called again. "Whoever it is, let me hear your voice." Still there was no answer.

For fear that whoever it was would do him harm, he stayed in his bed. "I know I can't see you, but I have a God Who does see you. He not only sees what you're doing, but He's looking inside your heart too." There was silence in the hut. The person stood still wherever he was. Ngende's words seemed to take him by surprise.

"God's Word says that whatsoever a man seweth, that shall he also reap," Ngende called out, not knowing how close the thief was to him. "You may not have to pay for your crime tonight but you will pay for it some day. God says that in His Book."

"I'm sorry, Ngende," came the familiar voice. "I knew the church gave you some money to help you and I only wanted a part of it."

Ngende sat up in bed and threw his legs over the side.

"Is that you, Sesse?"

"It's me, Ngende. I'm sorry for what I have done. I'll leave now. I've not taken any of your money. Goodbye, Ngende."

Before Ngende could say another word the young man left the hut and disappeared into the darkness. He knew that tribal law requires imprisonment for anyone caught stealing.

Ngende got out of bed and quickly dressed. He felt his way to the door and went out into the cold night. There he prayed, "Father, help me to find Sesse. He needs You. Keep him from running away."

Without help it was difficult for him to make progress, but he knew the area well and started down the path leading out of the village. Step by step the blind man groped his way along. When he was out of hearing distance of the village, he began to call Sesse's name.

"If you hear me, Sesse, answer me. I won't do you any harm. I have some good news to tell you." He had no way of knowing that the young African lad was hidden in a nearby thicket.

"Do you hear me, Sesse?" he called again. "Answer me. I have some good news for you." Then came a timid response.

"Here I am, Ngende. Please don't report me."

Ngende's heart jumped within him. He reached out and took Sesse by the arm.

"Don't be frightened, Sesse. I know you meant me no harm. Listen to me. I want to give you some good news."

Ngende began, as he had done so many times, to tell the story of Jesus. While he spoke, the tears ran from his eyes as he told of God's love and how He sent His Son, Jesus, to die for the sins of the world. It was not the first time Sesse had heard the Gospel. In fact he had heard it many times. But Ngende was persistent that night.

"Jesus died for you, Sesse. He wants to save you. He wants to forgive you of your sins. You can accept Him as your Savior and have everlasting life right here on this path. Will you accept Him, Sesse? Will you accept Jesus into your heart?"

"But . . . but . . . I tried to steal from you," Sesse stammered. "Why should you even care for me enough to come look for me and tell me about Jesus?"

"Because God loves you, Sesse," the old man answered. "Remember what I said to you there in my hut? I couldn't see you but God saw you and God not only saw what you were doing, Sesse, but He also knew what you were thinking. God looks into our hearts, too. We can't hide anything from Him."

"Will God forgive me of all my sins?" Sesse asked.

"Yes, He will, Sesse, but first of all you must ask Him to do it. Ask Him, Sesse, to forgive you of your sins. Ask Him to make you His child by faith in Jesus."

There on the path the two Africans had bowed their heads as Sesse confessed his sins and asked Jesus to save him.

When Ngende finished telling his story, Nan, whose eyes were filled with tears, looked across at her husband. Jim reached out and took Ngende by the hand.

"Thank you, Ngende, for being concerned about the lost, even for one who entered your house to rob you."

"That's what it's all about, Mr. Williams," replied the blind man. "Besides, I'm sure it was so dark out there, that Sesse couldn't see where he was going either. He told me later that was why he stopped to wait for the morning light. The Lord used my blindness as a means to reach Sesse with the Gospel."

"One more word," said Ngende, smiling. "There will be three of us in church, Sunday. Don't you think it's about time there's a place reserved for me and the new Christians in my village?"

Jim looked over at Nan and winked.

"I think you're right, Ngende. In fact, I'll speak to Pastor Gilbert today about your request."

In his mind, Ngende visualized an entire bench filled with converts from his village.

15

God
Turned
Him
Around

Bill Kemp hastily tore open the envelope to see what his missionary co-worker, Paul Benson, was writing about. Quickly his eyes scanned over the page.

"Bob and I would like to come over to your area to do some hunting. We are scheduled for a large pastor's conference here at the mission station in a few weeks and we would like to have a good supply of dried meat to help feed the out-of-town people who will be attending the conference. Knowing how you like to hunt, perhaps you could help us get something. Please let me know either by mail or by runner if it is all right for us to come and when would be the best time."

It was already the fifteenth of April and even though the dry season had another two months to go, the one seasonal mango rain, as the Africans called it, had wet the ground sufficiently enough two weeks before to bring forth a green carpet of new vegetation. Bill knew that it would be a good time to hunt the African game. With supplies running low, he and Nan decided to make the sixty-eight mile trip to the small town where Paul Benson and Bob Gilly taught in the national Bible school. Bill and Nan usually made a trip every six weeks to purchase supplies. With the mail service being so undependable, and wanting to get word to Bob and Paul as soon as possible, they thought it best to simply advance their shopping trip by two weeks.

Paul and Bob returned with Bill and Nan that same week to the small mission station located deep in the bush. It was too late in the day to do any hunting. After the evening meal they decided to clean their guns and make last minute checks of ammunition, water canteens, first-aid box, snake venom serum, etc. Since Bob did not own a gun of his own, Bill loaned him a 12-gauge shotgun, with a good supply of slugs.

The men talked late into the night about the mission work in general as well as their hunting trip the next day. Five o'clock in the morning seemed to come too quickly. Bill aroused his two friends and within a half hour they were in the pickup headed for one of Bill's favorite hunting places just five miles from the mission station. Several of the Christian Africans who were noted for their hunting skills joined the missionaries.

It was quite light by the time the men entered the woods. Bill noticed a high level of excitement with his two missionary co-workers. They did not hunt as much as he did.

"What can we expect to see around here, Bill?" asked Paul in a whisper.

"All kinds of antelope, but remember, we are in cape buffalo territory and it wouldn't surprise me one bit if we should come across some of those big fellows."

The men walked for some fifteen minutes before they spotted their first game. It was a rather small antelope, weighing approximately 100 pounds. They decided to track it. They hadn't gone far until David, one of the Africans, came to Bill informing him that he had just spotted a solitary cape buffalo a short ways away. Without hesitation the men left the trail of the antelope and proceeded to where David had seen the buffalo.

"It was right down there," said David, pointing to a large open plain. The men were standing on a rise about 30 feet above the level open plain that stretched before them for about a mile.

"It can't be far," continued David. "There are no woods for it to hide in." This reminded Bill of an unwritten law which he had promised always to obey when hunting buffalo. Never shoot a buffalo unless there is a tree nearby to climb. He noticed there was not a tree on the open plain.

"I think I know where it is," said David, pointing to a small clump of fifteen-feet high elephant grass out in the middle of the plain. "It could very well be in that grass. What do you want to do, Mr. Kemp?"

The men all agreed that with three guns they should be able to stop one buffalo. They decided to walk out to the grass which was about a half-mile away. With guns ready, the missionaries, along with their African companions, walked across the open plain to the patch of grass. Upon reaching it, they all stood still and listened.

"He's in there," whispered David, hearing the crackling of the dried grass. The men then decided to walk slowly around the edge of the grass to see if the buffalo would come out on the other side. They walked for about thirty feet when David stuck his arm out in front of Bill.

"There he is, Mr. Kemp." The African pointed to a huge bull cape buffalo just fifty feet away. It was standing broadside to the men, looking out over the plain. It was decided that Bill would shoot first since he had the .375 high powered magnum rifle. Paul and Bob would then follow with Paul's 30-06 and Bob's 12-gauge shotgun. Bill's first shot hit the buffalo too far behind the front shoulder, sending it into a terrible rage. It ran out onto the plain about 150 feet, turned around and spotted the men.

The Africans, knowing the danger, disappeared into the grass. The giant beast pawed at the ground, snorted, lowered its head and started for the missionaries. All three guns blasted away at the charging ferocious beast. The 150 foot distance soon became 100 and then 75 and then 50 feet and still the buffalo came. The men found their mark and slowed the charging animal to give time enough for reloading. The buffalo had one thing in mind and that was to eliminate the men who represented his enemies. Some 30 feet away the big black bull staggered and fell.

Within seconds it was on its feet again, but this time walking away from the missionaries. The men fired away, hitting the beast wherever they could. Down it went for the second time.

"Shoot him behind the head, Bob," called Bill. The missionary made his way rapidly to the side of the downed buffalo and finished it off with a shot at the base of the skull. How thankful the three were when it was all over.

"God protected you," said David. "No buffalo ever turns its back on its target and walks away. All three of you could have been killed, Mr. Kemp. God made him turn around and walk away from you."

The men then proceeded to count the times they had hit the buffalo. "I can't believe that it took seventeen shots to do the job," said Bob, fingering the hot barrel of the shotgun. "He sure was a tough one."

"He was tough," added Bill. "Had he not turned around when he did, I hate to think what would have happened to us. Like David said, God turned him around."

16
Never
Too
Busy

The line of cars seemed endless as Bill waited for an opening to back out of the driveway. "This morning's traffic is unbelievable," he whispered to himself as he joined the heavy flow of automobiles along Cedar Road.

It had been four years since Bill and Nan Kinder arrived home from Africa after completing their fifth four-year term of service. When a position in the mission home office administration was offered to Bill, the middle-aged couple accepted this as God's direction for the next step of service for Him.

As Bill drove down Chester Avenue, he was deep in thought about the mission's summer apprenticeship program. "I hope we can get our twelve workers for England before the month is out," he thought out loud. He turned into the parking lot and guided his car into a parking place. Stepping out of the vehicle, he looked up to see Kate, one of the girls from the accounting department, walking by.

"Hi, Mr. Kinder! How are you this morning?"

"I'm just fine, thank you, Kate. And how are you this beautiful morning?"

The pretty office worker stopped to wait for Bill to catch up with her. "Did you hear that Dan and Betty arrived safely in Australia?"

Bill could see the excitement in Kate's face as she spoke. She and Betty were cousins.

"No, I hadn't heard, Kate. Did they call?"

"Yes, they did. They called my Uncle Ed and Aunt Harriet as soon as they arrived."

Bill held the door open for Kate as they entered the office building. She quickly made her way down the hall. "I'll see you later, Mr. Kinder. Morning prayer meeting is about to begin."

The mission executive put his briefcase in his office and hurried to the dining room where the office personnel met each morning for Bible reading and prayer. A half hour later, Bill returned to his office to begin his day's work. Mentally he had a number of projects lined up and he was anxious to get at them. Cindy, his secretary, greeted him and then went over some papers with him.

"Don't forget your column for the state paper, Mr. Kinder. Thursday is the deadline for mailing it."

"Thanks, Cindy. I want to get that done this morning if at all possible."

The veteran missionary sat down and looked at the picture of Nan on the right side of his desk. "Thank You, Lord, for Nan," he prayed softly. He thought of their thirty years together, with most of those spent in the heart of Africa. "Those were such wonderful years," he whispered, picking up his pen.

"I'm sorry to disturb you, Mr. Kinder," spoke the receptionist from the doorway, "but there is a young man here in the waiting room who wants to talk to someone about the Bible. Do you have the time to see him?"

Bill laid down his pen and followed the receptionist down the hall. There standing before the desk was a tall young man.

"Hello there!" said Bill sticking out his hand. "I'm Bill Kinder."

"It's a pleasure to meet you, Mr. Kinder. I'm Jim Daniels."

The men shook hands and Bill asked Jim to come to his office. "Please be seated, Jim. I'll close the door to give us some privacy."

After they were both seated, Bill asked Jim what he could do for him.

"Well, Sir," began Jim, "I got pretty lonesome in my room last night and decided to read from the Bible if I could find it. My mother gave me one years ago and I knew it was around somewhere. I finally found it and began to read. I read where Jesus is coming back again and that scared me. I believe that Jesus is God's Son and I knew that I wasn't ready to meet Him. I found your mission's name and address in the phone book and that is how I came to you."

"Tell me, Jim," asked the missionary. "The Bible says that all have sinned. Do you believe that includes you?"

"I know it includes me, Sir. I know I'm a sinner."

"The Bible also says that the wages or penalty of sin is death—eternal death—separation from God forever in the Lake of Fire."

"I believe that, Sir," responded Jim. "I want to know what I can do about it." As he spoke, Jim fingered the car keys he held in his hand. Bill could see he was nervous.

"Jesus died on the cross for you, Jim. He paid the penalty for your sins. If you believe that He did this for you and confess your sins to Him, He will save you and become your Savior."

"I do want Him to be my Savior, Sir. I really want to belong to God."

In a moment, the visitor and the veteran missionary slipped to their knees. "God," prayed Jim, "I'm a sinner and I ask You to forgive me of my sins. I believe that Jesus is Your Son and that He died for me. I want Him to be my Savior. God, please save me."

After the two men had prayed, Bill looked over at Jim. A broad smile spread across his face. "I believe it Sir. I'm saved. I know I belong to God."

"That's what God's Word says, Jim. In the book of Romans, chapter ten and verse nine we read, 'That if thou shalt confess with thy mouth the Lord Jesus, and shalt believe in thine heart that God hath raised him from the dead, thou shalt be saved.'"

"Thank you, Mr. Kinder, for the help you've been to me today."

"Well, Jim," answered Bill, "that's what my work is all about. I delight in telling people about Christ."

"That makes me think of something I have to do."

"What do you mean, Jim?"

"You see, Sir, I'm a member of a gang here in the city. Those fellows need to hear about Christ. I must tell them what He has done for me."

"You are correct, Jim. You have a tremendous responsibility to tell others what Christ has done for you and what He can do for them."

Bill gave Jim some literature as well as the address of a sound, fundamental church. The two men shook hands out on the street. "You need to start attending a church that believes and teaches the Word of God. The church listed on the paper that I gave you is that kind of a church. The people are friendly and you will feel right at home there."

"Thank you, Mr. Kinder. I really appreciate your interest in me.

How desperately I needed someone to tell me about Jesus."

As Bill watched Jim walk down the street, he felt good inside. The work still lay unfinished on his desk and there were deadlines to meet, but somehow he wasn't too concerned. He knew that God had directed Jim Daniels to him.

"How glad I am," he thought, "that I wasn't too busy to tell that young man about Christ."

17

Did
God do
Something?

(as told by Sherry Claypoole)

"Hello, Sherry! How are you?"

The voice on the other end of the line indicated that my missionary co-worker had a problem.

"Dr. Kendrick, do you know of someone from this area who is going to the regional conference in Annandale (Virginia) who would have room for me to ride with them?"

"I can check and see, Sherry. What's the problem?" I asked, hoping to come up with some kind of solution.

"It's my car," she answered. "I've been told it has a burned valve. I know something is wrong with it because it doesn't have much power going up hill."

An idea flashed through my mind. If Sherry's car could make it to Annandale, perhaps there would be a mechanic in the church who could work on the car during the conference. If that wasn't possible, then someone there could at least direct her to a good garage.

"You have only good highways between your home and Annandale," I told Sherry after sharing my plan. "Stay by your phone and I'll call the church to see if something can be worked out. The conference is four days long and I'm sure that if we are able to get it into a garage right away, that will be time enough to fix it."

As soon as I hung up talking with Sherry, I called the church in Annandale. After explaining Sherry's problem to the church secretary, I was informed that she would make some telephone calls and get back with me. Within ten minutes she called me.

"Dr. Kendrick, I can't reach the man we have in mind, but the men here in the office told me to tell Sherry to bring her car down. They are sure that something can be worked out."

Sherry answered the phone after the first ring. "I think I can make it that far," she said. "I will call the church and tell them when I expect to arrive."

Because of a very tight schedule, it was necessary for me to take a plane to the conference. I thought of Sherry as I traveled, wondering how she was doing. The trip from Sherry's home town near Pittsburgh to Annandale would take a good part of the day even in a trouble free car. I wondered if I had given my co-worker good advice.

Upon my arrival at the church in Annandale on Saturday afternoon, I was glad to see that Sherry had arrived without any difficulty. Arrangements had been made for Sherry to put her car in the garage on Monday morning.

"Thank the Lord, Sherry," I said shaking her hand. "I was really concerned about you coming that distance."

In discussing the problem among ourselves, word got out among the church family of Sherry's car problem. Two high school seniors, Paul and Ken, who loved to work on cars and who had some used equipment in Paul's parents' garage, informed Paul's mother that they would like to take the job. Sherry heard about their offer from the church secretary on Sunday. Not knowing the boys or their mechanical abilities, Sherry didn't know what to say.

"I don't know what to do," said Sherry to several people standing nearby. "I'm sure the car needs repair. It didn't run right all the way here yesterday."

"I wouldn't hesitate at all to let those boys get into that engine," said one of the men from the church. "They know what they are doing."

The young missionary gave her consent for the two students to try their skills on her car. As soon as the boys heard of Sherry's decision, they began to work immediately on her car. Their testing equipment confirmed what the mechanic had told Sherry back in Pennsylvania.

"In fact," said Sherry that night at the church, "the fellows say there are three valves that are bad. Paul said one cylinder has no compression at all. I guess it's a miracle I ever got here."

Paul and Ken wasted no time. When they got home from church Monday night, they moved the car into Paul's parents' garage and to see that it would take more time than they had originally thought. Realizing that they had to go to school in the morning and their high school graduation was only a week away, they reluctantly decided that the job was too much for them. They could not see how they could have the car ready by Thursday morning.

Tuesday noon at the church, Sherry heard the disappointing news from Paul's mother.

"I regret to tell you this, Sherry," said the apologetic woman, "but after getting down to the problem last night, the boys decided it was just too much for them to do. They would have to send some of the work out to be done and with their graduation practices and other things facing them, there isn't time to get it ready for you by Thursday morning.

Sherry's heart sank.

"I appreciate their effort to help me," she responded. "Just tell them to put it back together and I'll try to find a garage someplace where it can be repaired."

Tuesday night after church the boys worked hard to get the car back together. About one o'clock the next morning they finished their work. Exhausted, discouraged and sleepy, they decided to take it for a short run to see that everything was working properly. It surprised them when the car started immediately. The two students couldn't believe the difference in the sound of the engine. The motor ran smoothly as they drove out onto the main street.

"Let's try the hill and see what it will do there," said Ken, his voice showing his excitement.

To the surprise of both the boys, the car took the hill with ease. There was no sign of any valve trouble. In fact, there wasn't one sign of any trouble.

"This is unbelievable, Ken," said Paul as they turned around at the top of the hill. "We know there are supposed to be burned valves in there but it doesn't act like it now."

They drove back to the house. Even though the hour was late, they wanted to share the good news with Paul's parents.

"Come on, Ken," said Paul laughing. "This is too good to keep from Mom and Dad."

"It runs like new, Mom," said Paul, grinning from ear to ear.

"And we really didn't do a thing to it," added Ken, with a puzzled look.

They both stopped, stared at each other and then looked at the two surprised parents.

"Mom," spoke Paul, "do you suppose that God did something in that engine?"

"Well, I know Sherry has been praying about this. And you know that Dad and I have been praying about it. Yes, Paul, I'm sure God did do something. I think we have seen a miracle."

The next morning Sherry called a number of garages to see if one of them could take her car to work on it. Having no success, she decided to go over to the church for the morning conference sessions. There she met Paul's mother.

"I'm sorry for all the trouble I caused the boys," Sherry began. "I've called several garages this morning but no one can take the car."

The lady smiled as she spoke.

"This sounds crazy, Sherry, but I don't think you'll have to take your car to a garage to get it fixed."

Sherry looked puzzled.

"You see, the boys took it out for a run early this morning. They tried it on a steep hill near the house and they say it runs perfectly."

Sherry stared at her friend in amazement. "You mean it runs all right? They didn't do anything to it?"

"That's right, Sherry. Paul and Ken didn't do a thing to it except to take it apart and put it back together."

"The Lord did it," said Sherry, slowly nodding her head.

"That's just about what Paul said when they brought the car back to the house this morning," added the happy mother.

Sherry went with one of the men of the church to get her car. She knew it sounded better the moment she heard the motor.

"You drive it, Sherry," the man from the church said. "I want you to try it out on the hill."

Before starting up the grade the man told Sherry to turn on her air conditioner.

"The car runs beautifully," said the happy missionary as the car climbed up the hill without any trouble.

Sherry Claypoole left Annandale on Thursday morning. She drove to North Carolina for her meetings and then on to Florida. While in Florida, she thought she would have a mechanic check the engine. She told him what had taken place in Annandale, Virginia.

After making careful tests, the Christian spoke to the missionary. "Sherry, you haven't got any engine problems. Whatever the boys did, it must have been right."

"I can answer Paul's question," said Sherry, smiling. "It was God. He did do something!"

18
A
Concrete
Answer

The missionary nurse looked up from her crouched position. The disturbed look on her face showed her deep concern for the young girl sitting on the ground before her.

"I wish we could do something about those chiggers in the church. That dirt floor is infested with them." She pointed to the girl's feet as she spoke. "I think all the children and most of the adults who come to church are infected with them."

Judy Smith had recently returned to Africa for her fourth term of service. Her previous twelve years experience of nursing gave her considerable knowledge of diseases and insects of the land.

Carefully taking in everything that Judy was saying was Gretchen Pile, a summer apprentice who had accompanied Judy back to the field just one week before. Gretchen would be entering her senior year in Bible college in the Fall. She was interested in missionary nursing and had applied to the mission for the Summer Apprenticeship Program.

"What are they, Judy?" asked the pretty college student bending over to have a closer look at the girl's feet. "What are those white areas?"

"Those are egg sacks," responded the missionary nurse. "When taken out, they leave quite a hole. I've seen toes completely destroyed because of so many egg sacks."

Judy then explained how the chiggers, which lived in the dirt, would get on exposed bare feet and without causing any pain, penetrate the skin and lay their eggs. As the eggs developed, the sacks would increase in size and eventually be discovered. They would then be dug out by the African with a pin or even a thorn. A continuation of infected feet would eventually permanently scar them.

"Are they in the church floor more than they are in other places?" Gretchen inquired.

"For some reason, they are not found everywhere. They seem to like loose dirt and the church floor is just that," Judy answered. "What we need is a concrete floor but the cost of one is definitely prohibitive with the funds with which we have to do our work."

That evening, Judy and Gretchen were invited to the home of Bill and Edna Taylor for a meal. Both girls spoke about the chiggers and the damage being done to the feet of the Africans. Both Bill and Edna mentioned the importance of having a concrete floor in the church. "Let's all pray and ask God to supply the funds for the floor," said Bill. "I would be only too glad to put it in if we can get the funds to do so."

"How much do you think it would cost, Bill?" Judy asked her co-worker.

Bill figured on a piece of paper for a couple of minutes and finally answered. "I believe $1,000 would do it. The funds would have to arrive soon, however, as I would have to get the sand out of the river before too many more rains."

"Why don't you start getting the sand out now, Honey?" Edna asked with her ever pleasant smile. "Let's take a step of faith and trust the Lord to send in those funds. Certainly the floor is needed!"

The missionaries banded together for special times of prayer for the need of funds. The African Christians, hearing about their missionary friends' prayer meetings, began their own prayer groups.

Judy and Gretchen were at the dispensary one morning when the local village chief came to have his ulcerated leg treated. His pointed teeth showed as he spoke. "God is going to give us a concrete floor, Miss Smith. My men are already digging sand from the river and we are organized to help Mr. Taylor to put in the floor when the load of cement arrives from the capital."

"But Mr. Taylor hasn't even ordered the cement yet, Chief Sesse," responded the surprised nurse. "We need money to do that."

"Well, I'm going to tell Mr. Taylor to order it right now because I know that God will supply the money. After all, that's no problem with Him," spoke the village leader.

The next day, the mail brought an unexpected letter from a person in Indiana. It was addressed to Judy. The lady wrote, "For several years I have followed your work with great interest. Ever since you showed your slides and spoke at our church, I have prayed daily for you and your ministry. A month ago, God called my dear husband home to be with Him. I just received his small insurance check. God has laid it upon my heart to give you $800 for you to use any way you wish there in the work. Perhaps there is a special need at this time."

Within the hour, the good news of the $800 gift was shared with Judy's co-workers. Chief Sesse stopped by the dispensary to see one of the patients and was thrilled to hear of the large gift.

"It's all going to be used for the floor," Judy said to the village chief. "Now, we must continue to pray for the other $200."

"It will come in, Miss Smith," spoke Chief Sesse in a confident tone. "My men are anxious to get to work on the floor. They already have a large pile of sand on the river bank."

Bill Taylor was in his office preparing some sermon notes when he heard someone clapping their hands outside. Opening the door, he saw Chief Sesse standing there with a broad smile on his face.

"Hello, Chief Sesse," said Bill reaching out to shake his friend's hand. "Come on in."

Before the chief even sat down, he began to talk. "Mr. Taylor, I'm here to give you a message from God."

Bill tried to hide the amused look on his face. He loved the way the Africans expressed themselves.

"What is the message that you have to give to me, my brother?"

"It is simply this, Mr. Taylor. God wants you to order the cement now without any further delay. He has told me that the money will be supplied. My men already have a large supply of sand out on the river bank."

Bill knew that God was at work in the hearts of the people. He, too, must trust the Lord for the remaining funds. That afternoon he wrote a letter to the mission's business man at the capital.

It was just two weeks to the day that Chief Sesse asked Bill to order the cement that the large transport truck arrived with its precious cargo of cement. The excited Africans gathered around the truck like a swarm of bees. Within an hour, all the bags of cement were neatly stacked in a nearby storehouse. Several of the women hastily prepared food for the truck driver to show appreciation for his part in transporting the cement. Chief Sesse climbed up onto the back of the truck and raised his arm for silence.

"Quiet Please!" he called out in a booming voice. "I have something very important to say to all of you."

Only the smacking lips of the driver could be heard as he enjoyed his meal. All eyes were on the village leader.

"We have suffered long enough from those tiny animals that live in the church dirt floor. They have made far too many holes in our feet."

The people clapped their hands to show their appreciation to what the chief was saying.

There is a need for a concrete floor. God answered part of our prayer by having a friend of Miss Smith give her $800 in American money. Mr. Taylor says that the concrete floor will cost $1,000 in American money. How much more do we need in American money to have enough to pay for our floor?"

"We need $200 more, Chief Sesse," called one of the school children.

"You're right, Samuel," responded the chief, "and right here in my pocket are enough franc notes to make up the $200. Several of you out there hearing my voice came to me in secret and gave me money from your cotton sales this year. Little did you realize that you were not the only one to do that. God worked in just the right number of hearts to give. The amount is perfect."

A loud clicking of tongues could be heard throughout the crowd.

Chief Sesse continued. "You have allowed yourselves to be God's answer along with the friend of Miss Smith who lives in America. We will soon be able to sit in church with our feet protected from these tiny animals by our new concrete floor."

One of the men began to sing, "Praise God from Whom all Blessings Flow." Others joined in and a beautiful song of praise was voiced by the entire group of villagers. Judy glanced over at Gretchen to see how the new apprentice was reacting to this unscheduled meeting. The pretty student stood in silence wiping the tears from her face. Her eyes twinkled with joy and a broad smile spread across her face as she turned to look at Judy.

"I love these people, Judy," she said softly. "I really love these people."

19

The
Dogwood
Tree

The screeching of brakes along with the sound of a sickening thud sent Martha Walton scurrying to the kitchen window overlooking the backyard. She gasped when she saw that the gate was open and little five-year-old Tammy was gone. The panic-stricken mother turned and raced through the house and out onto the front porch. The sight on the street made her legs feel like rubber as she ran down the steps across the lawn to the small pink-clad figure lying motionless on the road in front of a stopped car. Several other people who saw the accident happen had already made their way to the side of the still form. Standing close by her was her fluffy white toy poodle, Dogwood.

"Get an ambulance, somebody!" cried the frenzied mother as she cupped her hands gently about Tammy's blond curled head. "Oh, please, somebody, get help," pleaded Martha.

A short, pleasant-looking man knelt beside her and began to examine the little girl. He talked as he worked.

"I'm Dr. Hastings from Metro Hospital. I'm on my way home from work. The emergency unit has been called and should be here within minutes."

The presence of the physician gave Martha a measure of calmness which she desperately needed at that moment.

"How bad is she, Doctor?" inquired the young mother.

"I don't know," responded the physician. "We'll have to get that report later from the hospital."

Within fifteen minutes, Tammy, along with her mother and Dr. Hastings, were in Metro Hospital where the little girl was being examined to determine the extent of her injuries. One of the neighbors called Tom Walton at his office to inform him of the accident. He arrived minutes after his daughter entered the operating room. The tall businessman, upon entering the hospital, hurried to the side of his wife. The relief at seeing her husband opened the flood gates for the distraught mother. The past twenty minutes had been a nightmare she would never forget and at that moment their entire future seemed clouded with uncertainty. The life of their little girl hung in the balance.

Tom Walton was a man totally dedicated to his work. He spent time with his family and was a good husband and father. God, however, had no place in his life. He regularly drove his wife and little girl to church and picked them up after the services without ever complaining. He made it clear on more than one occasion that Martha could do as she pleased as far as church and God and that he would never interfere.

Martha Walton was saved one year after she and Tom were married. A nearby neighbor lady led her to Christ while she was visiting one day in the Walton home. Martha immediately began attending church on a regular basis. It was in the third year of their marriage when Tammy was born. Martha was a faithful wife and mother. She was a radiant testimony for the Lord.

"I wonder how she is," whispered Martha, squeezing Tom's hand. Without waiting for a response, she bowed her head and softly prayed.

"Dear Father, our Tammy belongs to you. We love her more than anything else in this world. Please, Lord, let her live. But if it is Your will to take her . . .," Martha halted as she wept. After a moment she continued. "If it is your will to take her, Lord, then that is all right, too. Everything You do is for our best."

Tom Walton knew that his wife's faith gave her some strong principles, but never did he realize how much she loved her God and desired His will to be done than at that moment. His eyes swelled with tears as he thought of his precious little girl lying motionless before the medical team which now worked on her. He thought of her dressed in that very same pink dress sitting on his lap singing her favorite song to him, "Jesus Loves Me." If his own sweet little daughter could love Jesus and live for Him at that early age, what was wrong with him.

"I've been so foolish, Martha," said Tom in a broken voice. "I've turned my back on God and I know He has caused this to happen to bring me to this point in my life. Honey, I need Jesus as my Savior like you and Tammy know Him."

In the quietness of the little room where Tom and Martha sat, clutching his wife's hand, Tom prayed, asking God to forgive him of his sins and to save him.

Dr. Hastings appeared in the doorway. A solemn look was on his face. He walked across the room and took Martha by the hand. He laid his other hand on Tom's shoulder.

"I'm sorry," he said. "We did all we could do. She never regained consciousness."

Tom looked up at the physician. Both men were weeping. "We understand, Doctor. We really understand. Thank you."

The funeral for Tammy Walton was attended by more than three hundred people. Tom gave a moving testimony at the service. Several indicated their need for Christ. Two days later, Tom and Martha stood in the backyard, looking at the place where Dogwood, Tammy's little dog, had dug the hole under the fence. A next door neighbor told them how she had seen Tammy open the gate and run quickly into the street after her dog. The driver of the car could not avoid hitting her. The white, fluffy toy poodle stood at their feet as they talked. Martha reached up into the blossoming dogwood tree and picked off one of the flowers. She looked at the white petals in her hand.

"She loved this tree, Tom. Do you remember how she told us she wanted to have her dog have the tree's name? She would play by the hour with her little table and chairs under it."

"I remember, Honey. This is her tree and those beautiful white petals will always remind me of our precious little Tammy." Tom hesitated and then continued. "God used her life and death to bring her daddy to trust Him."

20
Jim's Mission Field

The light of the campfire reflected on the faces of the campers. Bud Stern stood with his open Bible as he spoke to them. Throughout the week, the visiting missionary challenged the senior high school students to live for Christ. Now, this was his last opportunity to speak to them. Unconsciously, Bud searched for the face of Jim Hill. He would long remember the events involving himself and the high school senior through which developed a good friendship.

Bud had arrived on Monday about ten o'clock in the morning so he could decorate the chapel auditorium with his African curios before the campers made their appearance. After an early lunch with the staff, he returned to the chapel to finish his task.

The first of the campers arrived around two o'clock. Bud was on a step ladder putting the last thumb tack into the tail of a 19 foot python snake skin when three young men walked into the auditorium.

"Hey, look you guys, we're going to have some fun this week," spoke one of the boys. He purposely brushed against the table knocking a box of thumb tacks on the floor.

He looked up at Bud. "This stuff belong to you?" A sneer spread across his face as he glared at the missionary.

"Right!" answered Bud. "It's all mine. I brought two foot lockers filled with curios to show to you campers this week."

"Where did you get it?" demanded the teenage youth picking up a crude looking garden hoe to examine it.

"I brought it home from Africa," answered Bud stepping down to the floor. "You see, I'm a missionary from Africa. My wife and I have been there for the past twelve years."

"I've heard about missionaries," continued the young man, "but I've never seen one before. You mean you're from Africa?"

"That's right," answered Bud. "By the way, what are your names?"

Bud reached out to shake hands with his visitors.

"Jim," responded the youth. "Jim Hill. I came with these friends of mine. One of the guys went to church last Easter and picked up a paper about this camp. We decided to come and have some fun."

"I take it that you fellows don't go to church regularly," said Bud.

"Church!" responded Jim, sounding surprised at the question. "The place would fall down if I walked in."

"But you've come to a church camp," spoke the missionary.

"Hey, Jim," said one of the boys, "this place is not for us." The three boys broke out laughing and started toward the door.

Just then, Ed Brooks, the camp director walked into the chapel. "Hi, Bud. Just checking to see if you need any help. The campers are arriving and I knew you wanted to have everything in place before they came."

"Thanks, Ed," Bud answered. "I was just tacking up the tail of the python skin when these fellows walked in. We've been doing some chatting."

Bud glanced at a pack of cigarettes in one of the boy's pockets. Ed shook hands with the three men. He, too, noticed the cigarettes.

"Since you fellows are new here at camp, how about coming up to my office," requested the director. "I have some things to tell you." Ed glanced at Bud. "Since you've finished your decorating, Bud, and you already know the fellows, maybe you would like to join us."

Catching Ed's cue, the missionary walked along with Ed and the three youth. Once inside the office, Ed closed the door so he and Bud could talk to the boys in private.

"This is a Christian camp," began Ed. "Nearly all our campers come from churches. They came to have fun but also to hear messages from the Bible. Rev. Stern is the camp missionary for this week."

The boys' faces showed their surprise in finding themselves in such a situation.

Ed continued. "Every camper must attend all services. We also have rules forbidding smoking, drinking alcoholic beverages as well as using profane and other bad language."

He stopped for a moment and continued. "Now you can leave or stay. What do you want to do?"

"I'm leaving," spoke two of the boys together. Jim Hill remained curiously silent.

"What about you, Jim?" asked Ed.

The tall youth looked at his two friends. He thought for a moment and then spoke. "Look, you guys, go ahead and leave. I think I'll stay. I'll tell you all about it when I see you on Saturday. If I want to come home early, I'll give you a ring."

Jim then reached into his side pocket and pulled out a pack of cigarettes. "Might as well take these with you, Dan. You guys can take my smokes for me this week. No one's going to say that Jim Hill copped out of something because of religion. I can beat that, too."

Jim was assigned to a cabin with Ray Foss, a baseball and basketball star from a Christian college. This was Ray's third year as counselor at the camp. He was a bit taller and heavier than Jim which immediately gained him some respect from the camper.

That night after the evening meal, Bud spoke to the high school group. Jim was spellbound as he listened to the missionary tell about some of his experiences in Africa. He told how some of the people suffered and died for their faith in Christ. When he described how a seventeen year old Christian boy was buried alive upside down because of his love for Jesus, Jim felt a lump in his throat. His eyes became misty as Bud spoke. He had never heard of anything like that before.

"Andrew died for Christ," said Bud in a serious tone. "Some of you sitting here can't even live for Him."

The missionary pointed his finger at the group. "Listen, you fellows. It takes a real man to be the Christian that God wants him to be."

Jim didn't understand the strange feeling inside him. Why did the missionary's words effect him so much? Could he do what Andrew did? "But, I don't even know Jesus like that," whispered Jim to himself.

All of a sudden there was a great longing in Jim's heart to know more about Christ. When Bud asked those to stand who would like to be saved or know more about the gospel, Jim immediately stood up. He touched his face with his fingers and was surprised to find tears. Jim Hill was crying.

Ed Brooks gave Jim permission to go to the speaker's cabin to talk with the missionary and they talked long into the night. When Jim returned to his cabin about midnight, Ray laid awake waiting for him. The two shook hands when Jim entered the cabin. The counselor knew something wonderful had happened.

"I'm saved, Ray," said Jim smiling. "Jesus is my Savior. I know what it's all about now."

For the first time that Jim could remember, he fell asleep happy. He knew that his sins were forgiven and he was now a child of God.

The next morning in the Bible hour, Jim gave his testimony. After he finished, three fellows and two girls indicated by raised hands that they, too, wanted to be saved. It was only a sample of what was to take place for the next four days of camp.

The camp fire service the last night of camp was always the highlight of the week. The fire blazed bright as Bud spoke to the young men and women.

"God has performed many miracles in camp this week."

The campers nodded their heads in agreement.

"There have been 19 professions of faith in Christ and 23 others have made decisions to dedicate their lives to the Lord for His service."

Bud looked over at Jim. "I've asked Jim Hill to share something with you before we close our camp fire service."

The new Christian stood up and nervously cleared his throat. "Well, I thought I came here by mistake. I know now that it wasn't a mistake. God doesn't make mistakes. I didn't know what to expect except I thought I would stir up some trouble. Rev. Stern here and Mr. Brooks and Ray Foss soon made friends with me and kind of took over."

The campers laughed at Jim's remarks causing him to relax a bit.

"My first night here, I got saved. I don't think I'll ever forget hearing Rev. Stern tell about how Andrew died because of his faith in Jesus. When I heard about that, it did something inside of me. I knew then, that all of this about Christ must be real."

Jim choked up as he continued. "And it is real, friends. It's real because it happened to me. Jim Hill is different and I can promise you that I want to live for Christ the rest of my life."

When Jim finished, many of the campers had tears in their eyes. There was absolute silence as he made his way back to the log where he sat down. One by one, the young people stood to testify. The spirit of revival swept the little group. At midnight, they returned to their cabins. The next day they would be returning home.

Bud stretched from the top step of the ladder to unhook the tail of the snake skin. The door of the chapel opened and he heard a familiar voice. "Hey, look you guys, we're going to have some fun this week." There below Bud was Jim Hill looking up with a big smile spread across his face.

"Remember those words, Rev. Stern?" he asked.

"I sure do, Jim," responded Bud. "And we did have some fun, didn't we?"

Minutes later, the two friends shook hands before Jim left for the waiting car outside. "Pray for me, Rev. Stern. My first job for the Lord is to see that my unsaved friends there in that car hear about Jesus."

He pointed to the car where his two friends waited. "That's my mission field, Rev. Stern. I'll be sure and write and tell you what happens."

Bud watched the car until it disappeared. "Lord," he prayed, "help Jim to witness to his friends. Give him the joy of leading them to Christ."

21
Just
in
Time

What's that noise, Daddy?" asked nine-year-old David sitting in the back seat. "It sounds like we are running over bumps."

Henry glanced into the rearview mirror as he responded to David's question. "It's a bubble on one of our back tires. I'm going to stop at the next station to see if we can buy a new tire."

Five minutes later, the little family stopped at a gas station, only to find it had no tires to fit the car.

"There's another station ten miles to the West," spoke the station owner. "I'm sure you will find tires there."

"Tires!" repeated Henry, "I want only one."

"You need two tires, Sir," answered the stranger. "Your other back tire has a large split in it. You had better get two while you're at it."

"Could we stop for a bite to eat, Henry?" asked Beth as they started out again. "I'm afraid if we get tied up at a garage, it will be rather late to stop for our lunch."

"There's a sign now," said Henry pointing to a large billboard. "How does a hamburger and french fries sound?"

"Sounds good to me, Dad," answered David enthusiastically.

"Sounds good to me, too," echoed Beth. "I don't think I will get tired of hamburgers for a long time. I sure missed eating in places like this while we were in Africa."

The problem with the tires was forgotten momentarily as the Harper family enjoyed their lunch. "This sure is a good shake," David offered between gulps.

It had been three months since the Harpers had returned from their second term of service in Africa. Now they were working their way to the West Coast.

In a short time they were on the highway again well aware of their tire problem. "I hope they have tires our size," spoke Henry, heading onto the exit ramp. He could see the large garage a short distance ahead.

"They have a special on tires, Henry," Beth said, pointing to a sign in front of the station. "It says two for $75 including balancing and mounting."

A young man appeared in greasy coveralls. "Can I help you, Sir?"

"I would like to buy two tires," Henry said stepping out of the car. "Can you put them on right away?"

"My boss is gone for a little while, Sir, but I'll do my best. I take it you want our special?"

"Yes, I do," responded the veteran missionary. "I'll help you mount them if you wish."

"Oh, I think I can do it all right. There's no sense for you to get all dirty. I will have to use tire irons because our changer machine is broken."

Henry watched as the young man struggled with the unfamiliar irons. The missionary's experience in Africa told him the lad needed help.

"I think I had better help you," said Henry finally. "We have to reach Des Moines by evening in order to look for a motel."

"There's a motel right down the street, Sir, in case you want to stay here for the night."

"Thanks," answered Henry, "but I think we should try to make Des Moines tonight. You see, we're on our way to the West Coast and we must stick with our travel plans."

"Oh, no," said the young man as he began to take off the other wheel. "Now I've done it."

"What happened?" asked Henry going to where the station attendant was standing with the lug wrench.

"I broke off one of your wheel bolts. Don't worry, though, we will replace it for you but it will take some time to do it."

"Why don't you replace the bolt?" suggested Henry. "I'll put the new tires on the rims. By the way, what's your name?"

"Steve," answered the young man, "Steve Evans."

"OK, Steve," said the missionary picking up the tire irons, "I'll work on these tires if you don't mind."

Henry had the new tires on the rims within an hour and then went to help Steve who was having difficulty replacing the bolt. They were just about finished when a car drove into the station. A middle-age man stuck his head out the window. "How are things going, Steve? Need any help?"

"No, thank you, Mr. Perkins," answered Steve. "I just sold two tires to this man for our special price. They were the last two of that size, too."

"Where did you get them?" asked the station owner.

Steve pointed to the right side of the garage where there were several stacks of tires. "Right there in the corner, Sir."

"Oh, no," grunted the owner, "those are my expensive tires. They're $140 for two."

Henry felt sick in his stomach. "Did you say $140?"

"That's right. They're $140 a pair."

"But your sign says $75 for two with balancing and mounting," said Henry pointing to the large sign in front of the window.

"I'm sorry, Sir, but those tires are $140 for two. They don't happen to be the ones on special."

Henry and Beth knew that such a financial outlay would greatly cut into their savings for the trip. "We may as well pay it, Henry," said the young wife. "We need them and besides, they're already on the car. To wait and put two other tires on would delay us even longer."

"I really don't want to argue with the station owner, Honey," Henry responded. "I've been witnessing to Steve since we've been here and I want to witness to the owner, too, before we leave."

The missionary couple reluctantly paid their bill and in a short time was headed for Des Moines. "We should be there in about an hour," said Beth looking at her watch.

Henry noticed some black clouds off in the distance and pointed to them. "Those clouds don't look good," he said. "The wind is picking up, too."

The storm clouds gathered behind them as they continued on their way West. Henry watched them in the rear view mirror. "I'm glad we're not back there now. It looks like they're really having a bad one."

It was seven o'clock by the time the Harpers entered the outskirts of Des Moines. They immediately began searching for a motel. Beth looked over at her husband. "Do you know we spent more than three hours at that station?"

"We would still be there if I hadn't helped Steve," responded Henry. "It gave me a wonderful opportunity, though, to witness to him. He said he knew he should receive Christ but didn't want to do it just then."

"Like so many others," said Beth. "So near and yet so far."

"There's a motel," spoke David from the back seat.

A moment later, Henry pulled into the parking lot and went into the office. "We have one room left," said the lady at the desk. "We can put a cot in the room for your son."

"Thank You, Lord," prayed Henry under his breath as he filled out the registration papers. "I know You wanted us to stay here tonight."

Up in their room a short time later, David turned on the television while his parents freshened up a bit for the evening meal. "Hey, look!" he called pointing into the TV. "That's where we were this afternoon. Look! There's the station owner's car."

Henry and Beth raced to look at the picture on the TV. "It is his car!" said Beth pointing excitedly to where they had just been hours earlier. "The garage is gone, Henry. And look at the motel. It's only half there."

"That was a tornado we saw as we were leaving," spoke Henry with a serious look spread across his face. "We got away from there just in time."

"The thought of it sends the chills up my back," added Beth. "Surely, we would have been hurt or possibly killed had we stayed any longer."

"What about Steve, Dad?" asked David, sadly.

"And the station owner?" added Beth.

"We'll probably never know," answered the veteran missionary. "We do know they both heard the gospel today . . . and possibly for the last time, too."

Beth reached out and took her husband's hand. "You know, Henry, I'm glad we bought our tires there. It cost us more than we wanted to pay but it was worth every cent."

"I believe you're right, Beth," said Henry nodding his head. "I believe you're right."

After the news flash ended, the little family knelt beside the bed and thanked God for sparing their lives.

(Reprinted by permission of Regular Baptist Press)

22

One
Lone
White
Duck

(A true account)

It was just a lone white duck but everything about it captured my attention. Its unusual companions made the scene a very interesting one. What a combination they made. A duck and seven Canadian geese.

Their relationship was such that it was nearly impossible to separate them. The unique friendship challenged me to investigate the strange mixture.

The first thing I noticed was that the geese never failed to place themselves in strategic positions around their domesticated companion in order to protect it. Wherever the duck went, it was always surrounded by the wild geese.

Not wanting to scare the little flock, I carefully approached the feathered friends. It was my intention to try and separate the geese from the duck. The duck took off running at a rather slow pace. Its seven companions, which could run much faster or even take to the air if they chose, kept to the speed of the duck taking up their defensive positions as they moved along. They remained at their posts speeding up or slowing down responding to their friend's wishes until they reached the edge of the pond. There the geese stopped and allowed the duck to decide what it wanted to do. Into the water it went, heading out towards the center of the pond.

Again, they took up their positions but evidently, their defense on water was a bit different than that on land. The geese swam on each side of the duck as well as behind it. I watched them as they always were careful to maneuver themselves on both sides of their friend and between it and the nearest point of land. In no way, as far as they were concerned, was an enemy going to harm their companion.

One day I went to the pond early in the morning. I found the seven geese and lone duck at the shallow end of the pond. The geese had taken up their positions but this time in their land formation as the shores were close by. Each goose was in its place holding its head high while turning to look in all directions. To my amazement, the duck was fearlessly feeding on the vegetation at the bottom of the pond. I stood in silence as I took in the strange sight. What devotion exercised by those seven geese for their adopted friend.

The same day, I returned to the pond. This time I found the geese feeding on the grass along the shore while the duck patiently waited for them. As they moved about eating the grass, they made sure the duck was always situated in the center.

Perhaps one of the most unusual happenings was the flying exercise the geese were able to do even though they were committed to stay with and protect their slow moving, nonflying friend. I was nearing the pond one day when I heard the honking of geese. Surely, I thought, the geese did not leave the duck alone. As I approached the pond, there they were. The duck surrounded by five geese while the other two were taking their flying exercise. Upon their return to land to take up their positions by the duck, two other geese would leave for their turn of flying. I must confess that I stood in utter amazement as I watched the dedication of the seven Canadian geese to protect the duck.

Every now and then I'm reminded of the lone white duck and the geese. True, they are only fowls but what tremendous spiritual lessons they were to me.

I think of God's faithfulness as a true Friend. He said, "I will never leave thee, nor forsake thee." Heb. 13:5b. His protecting hand securely holds us every moment of the day and night.

Amidst the turmoils and dangers of this world, we can assuredly feed on His Word which gives us daily strength, comfort and encouragement. Without it, we become weak and are prone to temptations which constantly confront us. "Let the Word of Christ dwell in you richly, in all wisdom teaching and admonishing one another, in psalms and hymns and spiritual songs singing with grace in your hearts to the Lord." Col. 3:16.

What a wonderful truth to know that an infinite, righteous God loves unworthy, helpless, sinful, finite creatures like us. Nothing within us merits such heavenly love and concern. It is by His compassionate love. "For God so loved the world that He gave His only begotten Son . . ." John 3:16a. "For by grace are ye saved through faith and that not of yourselves, it is the gift of God." Ephes. 2:8.

Yes, a lone white duck and seven Canadian geese but lessons galore from their amazing devotion to each other. How much more should we, as people, exercise love, concern and devotion to each other and especially to our Heavenly Father.

(Reprinted by permission of Regular Baptist Press)

23

New
Truth

"**B**ut, Dad, we don't need fairy tales about Jesus anymore."

Sue's voice sounded a bit harsh as she spoke with her father who was sitting in his favorite easy chair. The expression on Ray Collins' face signaled his disbelief at what he had just heard from the lips of his seventeen-year-old daughter.

"What do you mean by that, Sue?" questioned the surprised father.

Sue picked at her high school ring as she spoke.

"It's just that I don't have to rely on Jesus any more, Dad. Those stories were all right while I was growing up, but now I don't need them."

Ray Collins was stunned to hear his daughter's words. It didn't sound like the same little girl who had memorized and loved so many of the well known Bible stories.

"It's true, Dad. I know this hurts you but I wanted you and Mom to know today how I feel. I'm not going to church tomorrow. In fact, I'm through going to church at all!"

Mary Collins entered the room just in time to hear her daughter announce that she was not going to church. She stood speechless as she listened to the unbelievable words.

"I . . .I . . .don't understand, Honey. What's happened?" asked her father.

"I've found new truth, Dad," answered Sue, looking away as she spoke.

"You've found what?" asked her father, a puzzled look spreading across his face.

"I've found new truth. I made up my mind about it last week. I. . .I. . .guess I was afraid to tell you and Mom, but since tomorrow is Sunday, I figured I had better tell you today."

"Honey," spoke her mother, "you really don't mean what you're saying, do you?"

Sue turned toward her mother. She noticed her trembling lips. She knew her words hurt her parents and this was something she didn't want to do.

"Sue," continued the middle-age woman, "you've known about Jesus since you were a little girl. You were singing about Him from the time you learned to talk."

"I know that, Mom, but I just don't believe that stuff about Him. That's for the kids who don't know any better.

Ray Collins stood to his feet. Slowly he approached his only daughter. He searched for words.

"Honey, tell me. What is the new truth? Where did you get it?"

"I got it in biology class, Dad. Mr. Smith can give you the best answers about it. I have my biology book up in my room if you want to look at it. It explains how the universe was formed and it tells where man came from, too. It's a lot different from what the Bible says— and makes more sense, too.

Before any more could be said, Sue turned and headed for her room.

"I have a report to get ready for biology. Besides, I don't want to talk about this any more."

Ray and Mary stood in silence as they watched Sue mount the steps to her bedroom. Unknown to them at the time, their daughter's life would take a turn from God, parents, home and church for the rest of the year.

It was an unusually difficult summer for the Collins. At first the people at the church asked questions regarding Sue's absence, but soon the word spread that she wanted nothing more to do with church or her Christian friends. She spent more and more time with her unsaved school friends. Some of the people at church who knew her well tried to talk with her, but were always turned away with a remark about Bible fables and the new truth she had found.

Seven months had gone by since Sue made her decision to stay away from church. She had graduated from high school and was a freshman in the nearby state college. It was seven days before Christmas and she was on her way home to spend the holidays with her parents. Fifty miles from home, it began to snow. The farther she drove, the more the snow accumulated on the road. It was difficult to keep the car from sliding and the thick, wet snow was too much for the windshield wipers.

"I'd better call Mom and Dad," Sue said to herself. "At this rate, I won't get home until very late." She saw lights up ahead.

"A gas station, I'll stop here and make my call."

Sue pulled into the station just as the attendant was locking the door.

"Sir," she called, "just a minute, please."

The attendant looked up to see the young lady step from her car.

"Do you have a phone I can use. I'm on my way home from college and am late because of this storm. My parents will be worried."

"Sure do," answered the attendant. "I was closing up for the night, but come on in. The phone's over there on the wall. This is a bad night for you to be out."

"Hello, Mom, this is Sue. I'm at a gas station three miles on the other side of Phillipsburg."

"Andrew's Service Station," said the attendant, tearing a wrapper from a candy bar.

"Hi, Dad . . . Yes, I'm all right . . . About six inches, but the radio report is for at least a foot more . . . Where am I? I'm at Andrew's Service Station. It's about three miles east of Phillipsburg . . . You want me to wait here?"

Sue looked at the attendant who pointed to a small store next door.

"Dad, I'll be in the store next to the station. All right? I'll see you soon. Love you."

"My dad is driving over with my brother, Paul, to get me. He doesn't want me to drive any farther alone," spoke Sue, looking out at the storm.

"He's wise, young lady. If you want to, you can leave your car under the shelter by the pumps. It will be safe there."

Sue walked over to the little general store and asked if she could wait there.

"We close at nine, but we live in the back of the store so you can stay as long as you want," said the elderly gentleman.

By ten o'clock Sue began to get worried about her father and brother. She called her mother to learn that her father and brother had left home three hours earlier. She gave her mother the telephone number of the elderly couple in case she had to contact her for some reason.

"It's a bad night, Honey," comforted the man's wife. "Can't go anywhere in this stuff."

Sue walked to the window and looked out, hoping to catch a glimpse of light on the road. A tear trickled down her cheek. She thought of the past seven months of her life. If only she could cry out to the Lord to help her. But then, would He hear her after all she had said about Him?

A lump was in her throat. She dabbed at her eyes with her handkerchief.

"If only Dad would come," she whispered. "I need to talk with him. I want to tell him I'm sorry for what I've said and done. I want Dad to pray with me like he used to do."

The ring of the telephone startled Sue. The store owner picked up the phone.

"Hello!. . .Who?. . .Sue? Hold on, she's right here."

"Hello," said Sue, her voice a bit shakey.

"Honey, this is Mom," came the voice through the receiver. Mary Collins' voice was at a breaking point. A cold chill swept over Sue's body. She knew something was wrong.

"Uncle Harry is coming to get you, Honey. Dad and Paul had an accident. Sue, I don't know how to tell you this. Your father was hurt seriously and is not expected to live."

Mary sobbed quietly while waiting for Sue to answer. The college freshman opened her mouth to speak, but no sound came forth.

"Is something the matter, Honey?" asked the storekeeper's wife as Sue hung up the phone.

"My dad," answered Sue in a daze. "He was in an accident coming to get me."

The plow trucks kept the roads open for emergency traffic. Harry Collins and a neighbor showed up after midnight. Sue's uncle told her of the accident that had happened only ten miles from home. A semi-tractor trailer went out of control and pinned her father's car against a concrete abutment. Her father was paralyzed from the waist down. Paul had a few minor cuts and a badly sprained ankle.

At 2:45 a.m. they pulled into the driveway. Mary Collins met her daughter at the door. Sue threw her arms around her mother. The two men stood silently as mother and daughter shared their grief.

The next few days were like a bad dream to Sue. She saw her

father at the hospital two days later. He was still too incoherent to talk with her. She wanted so very much to be able to correct the hurt she had caused him. Her heart ached as she thought of her past months of thoughtless living.

"Lord," prayed Sue that night in her room, "I've asked You to forgive me and I know You have done that. Thank You, Father, for my parents' love and forgiveness." Sue wept as she prayed.

"Thank You, Lord for the only truth, Your Word. Help me to know more about it so I can share it with others."

The next morning Sue was able to speak with her father for the first time since the accident. She told her parents she was not going back to the state college.

"God wants me to go to Bible college, Mom and Dad. I've got some time to make up and I want to begin right now."

Tears filled Mary Collins' eyes as she put her arms around her daughter and drew her close. Ray Collins reached out to take Sue's hand.

"Thank You, Father," whispered the happy mother, "for Your perfect will in our lives. You allowed this accident to happen, but through it You brought back our Sue."

"Thank You, Lord," echoed Sue.

Ray and Mary Collins knew their daughter had really returned.

(Reprinted by permission of Regular Baptist Press)

24
Starting
All
Over

The empty can falling off the bed startled Mark who sleepily reached for the switch on his bedside lamp. As the bright light flooded the room, reality once again gripped the heart of the young man. Crawling out of bed, Mark looked about at the disarray. Dirty clothes lay scattered around among the empty beer cans. A half bottle of whiskey was on top of the dresser. Cigarette butts were everywhere. Mark was desperate. Never before had he felt such a need for someone to help him.

It had been an exciting day for Pastor and Mrs. Bill Sommers. The time had arrived for the birth of their first child. The ladies at First Baptist Church gave generously in their baby showers for Jane. Everything was ready for the new baby's entrance into the world.

"It's a boy, Rev. Sommers," said the smiling nurse. "You have a fine looking boy."

A short time later the young preacher stood proudly looking at his new son.

"He looks like you, Bill," said Jane, squeezing her husband's hand. "I hope someday he'll be a preacher like his daddy." The young couple bowed their heads and, as they had done many times before Mark's birth, they committed their child to the Lord.

Mark grew up in the church family. As a baby, he attended Sunday School and church. He learned to say the name of "Jesus" almost as quickly as "Mommy" and "Daddy." When he was six years old, his mother had the joy one night, after she tucked him into bed, to hear him pray and ask Jesus to become his Savior.

As Mark grew physically, he also matured spiritually. Throughout his junior high and high school years, he was known for his Christian testimony by both faculty and students. Because of his sports abilities, Mark became the star player on both the football and baseball teams. It wasn't long before he was known as "preacher" about the school. Even the roughest students honored his Christian testimony.

Bill and Jane Sommers were thrilled that Sunday night when Mark walked forward in church to commit himself to go to Bible School.

"I feel so good inside," he said to them as they rode home after the service. "I just know that God wants me to go to Bible school and He knows my heart is open to Him to do His will."

What a blessed day it was for Bill and Jane as they took Mark to a Bible college in a neighboring state.

"Praise the Lord for His leading in your life, Honey," said the excited mother as she kissed her son good-bye.

"That's right, Mom," said Mark, with a lump in his throat. "I'm here because He has sent me. I know, too, that He has given me the best parents in the whole world."

Mark's first year in Bible college was filled with many blessings for the young man. His participation in street meetings and gospel teams caused even greater rejoicing in the hearts of his mother and father.

Halfway through his second year of Bible school the first hint appeared that all was not well. It came in a letter from Mark to his parents.

"I was called to the dean's office today because I skipped chapel. I didn't tell you before, but since I know you will find out anyway, this has been the third time I have been called in to see Mr. Woods."

Unknown to his mother and father, Mark had dropped from the gospel team in which he had been traveling. In order to get some spending money, he took a job in a restaurant in a nearby town, washing dishes. Working with him were several unsaved college students from the local secular college. Mark began to spend more and more time with his unsaved friends than he did with his fellow Bible students. Little by little he began to slip in his walk for the Lord. His church attendance fell off considerably. Bible reading, witnessing and Christian fellowship were something of the past.

Then one night after work, when he went to the movies with his friends, Mark took his first drink. They had just left the theater parking lot when they opened several cans of beer.

"Come on, Mark, one little taste isn't going to hurt you," said one of the fellows, shoving a can of beer into Mark's hands.

"Be a sport, Mark. After all, being sociable is good for you," added another.

Jokingly, one of the fellows pushed the can of beer to Mark's lips.

"Come on, Mark, take a sip."

Before he realized what had happened, Mark took his first drink of beer. Withing minutes he had emptied the can. As he stepped out of the car at the end of the college driveway, the fellows slapped him on the back, congratulating him for what he had done. Mark Sommers had not only violated several of the college's rules, but unknown to him, he had opened the door for increasing attacks from Satan on his life.

Bill Sommers stood speechless as he listened to the president of the Bible college.

"I'm sorry, Rev. Sommers, but it is necessary for us to expel Mark. He has been seen in a local bar and we have found alcoholic beverages in his room here at the college. I'm afraid Mark has been influenced by the wrong crowd, Rev. Sommers. It grieves me terribly to have to give you this news."

Later that day Mark's parents were able to contact him at school. They were shocked to hear their son's words.

"This place is a dump, Dad. There's no fun living here. I've wanted to leave anyway. The kids are just a bunch of holier than thou's."

Within two days Mark was home. Not only his attitude was changed for the worse, but his appearance as well. He just didn't look like the same Mark who went to Bible school two years before. During the second week he was home, he told his parents he was moving out.

"But where will you go, Mark? You don't even have a job," said his mother. Her voice shook as she spoke. She could imagine only the worst things happening to him.

"I'm going back to the restaurant, Mom. I know I can have a full time job there. Besides, my friends are there. I'll be able to stay with one of the guys until I can get my own room."

Overwhelmed with sadness, Bill and Jane said good-bye to Mark. Nothing they could say would change his mind. Their hearts ached as they drove back home from the bus station. They rode in silence for some distance before Bill spoke.

"We've done what we can, Honey. It's not that Mark doesn't know better. He does. All we can do is pray for him."

The days dragged into weeks. Mark's parents wondered how they could last another day. Their hearts seemed to ache continually. Then the phone call came. Mark wept as he spoke.

"I . . . I . . . can't go on this way, Dad. I'm so miserable. I just don't want to live!"

Bill and Jane talked for over an hour with Mark. The longer they talked the better he seemed to respond.

"I'll be there in the morning, Son," said his father. "Try to get some rest. I'm starting out now. It should take about seven hours to get there."

At nine o'clock the next morning the concerned father pulled up in front of a dingy looking apartment house. Mark waved from a window on the third floor. Immediately he met his father at the front door. The two threw their arms around each other.

"Dad," he cried, "am I ever glad to see you! I've done so much wrong. I've ruined my life."

Bill's eyes brimmed with tears.

"We love you, Son," spoke the weeping father. "You know you have our forgiveness and you know, too, the Lord will forgive you if you ask Him."

"I have asked Him, Dad," answered Mark. "I prayed a lot last night after I called you and Mom. I've got a lot to make up."

Mark had a small suitcase in his hand.

"This is all I'm taking with me. I cleaned out my room and have paid the landlord. I'm starting all over, Dad. I don't want anything around to remind me of the way I lived—not one thing."

Bill Sommers' heart was filled with praise as he headed back home. It would be a joy to help his son get started again.

(Reprinted by permission of Regular Baptist Press)

25
That
One
Cookie

"**C**ome on, Tom, eat one. It's not going to hurt you."

Tom Upland looked at his new neighbor, Eric Stenner, who was holding the package of chocolate cookies out to him.

"I can't Eric. You stole them from Mr. Frost. It would be wrong for me to eat one."

"You're a chicken, Tom Upland. Look, Old Man Frost will never miss them. He's got plenty more where these came from. Come on, be a sport."

"I'm sorry, Eric, but . . . I . . . I can't do it. It's just not right."

"O.K., Mr. Goodie, it's you that's missing out, not me!" Eric turned to walk away. "And about that invite to church, well, you can just forget it."

"But . . . but," stammered Tom as he followed after his enraged friend.

"You heard me, Upland, just forget it!"

The Stenners had moved into the neighborhood a week before. Eric was the first to meet the Upland family and spent a lot of time in their home. It was only that past Monday that Tom got up enough courage to invite Eric to go to church with him. Reluctantly, the new neighbor had agreed. Now, Tom thought he had ruined everything.

He called after his friend, "Eric, wait for me. I've got something to tell you."

"I said, forget it, Tom. You're too good for me."

Tom was desperate. He saw his opportunity to get Eric to go to church slipping away. Maybe if he took just one cookie. Surely the Lord would understand that.

"I've thought it over, Eric," said Tom, feeling a wave of guilt sweep over him. "If your offer is still good, I'll have a cookie, but only one, O.K.?"

"Do you mean it, Tom?" asked Eric, surprised, yet glad to hear his friend's decision.

"I. . .I mean it, Eric. But I'm taking only one."

Hesitantly, Tom reached out and took one of the cookies. Slowly he lifted it to his mouth. As he bit into the tasty chocolate, he felt terrible inside. Eric watched with a look of satisfaction on his face.

"That's more like it, Tom. It tastes pretty good, doesn't it?" Tom did not answer.

Eric continued. "I don't mind my friends having religion, but when you can't even eat a cookie, that's taking it too far. Now you're showing sense, Tom."

That night, Tom found it difficult to get to sleep. He could hardly believe that one cookie could cause him so much guilt. Each time he closed his eyes, he saw his hand reaching out to the box of cookies.

"Dear Lord," he prayed, "I only wanted Eric to go to church with me." The more he prayed the worse he felt. The minutes seemed to drag by. He watched the hands move slowly on his illuminated clock which sat on a bedside table.

"And all this because I ate a cookie," Tom whispered to himself. He finally drifted off into a deep sleep. Rays from the morning sun peeping over the distant hill found their way into Tom's room. A tiny bright spot focused on his face, causing him to wake up. Sleepily he rubbed his eyes. The smell of bacon told him it was time to get up. All of a sudden the thought struck him—the cookie he had eaten the night before! The guilty feeling returned.

"I'll talk to mom and dad about it," he said to himself. "I'm sure they will understand."

Tom decided the best time to speak with his parents would be after breakfast. In a short time, the little family sat down at the table.

"Tom," said his father, "would you thank the Lord for our food this morning?"

The three of them bowed their heads as Tom began to pray. "Dear Father," he said in a shaky voice, "thank You for the good night's sleep. Thank You, too, Lord for the food that. . .that. . ." Tom stopped and buried his head in his hands. "Dad," he said softly, "I can't pray. I just can't do it."

Ken Upland gently slipped his arm around his son. "What's wrong, Tom," he asked tenderly. "Is there something that's troubling you?"

Tom then told his parents how he had eaten one of the cookies that Eric had stolen. "I did it so he would go to church with me Sunday. At first, I said I wouldn't eat it. He became angry and walked away. He told me to forget the invitation. I decided to take one. I didn't want to lose out with Eric."

"You meant well, Tom," said his mother, "but many times, even though we mean well in the things we do, we still sin against the Lord."

"I know that now, Mom," said Tom. He turned to his father. "What can I do about it, Dad? Is there some way I can correct what I've done?"

Ken Upland looked into the pleading eyes of his son. "First of all, Tom, confess to the Lord what you've done. He'll forgive you. Then I would talk with Eric. Tell him how you feel about the whole thing. Don't be afraid to tell him the truth—that is, you have done wrong in the Lord's eyes."

"But what about Mr. Frost, Dad?"

"I was just getting to him, Tom," answered his father, with an understanding look on his face. "I suggest you go to see him as soon as possible. Tell him what you did and pay him for the cookies."

"I'll be glad to do that, Dad," said Tom. He was relieved to hear what his father had to say. He always seemed to have the right answer.

After breakfast, Tom went over to the Stenner's house.

"Why should you worry about eating a cookie?" questioned Eric, still puzzled over his friend's concern. "After all, I'm the one who stole them, not you."

"But . . . but it's wrong, Eric. You see, I'm a Christian and I know I've disobeyed the Lord. I was just as wrong in eating a cookie as you were in stealing them."

Tom paused a moment and went on. "Since I believe the Bible is God's Word, then I really should obey what it says."

The unsaved neighbor scratched his head as he thought about Tom's words. "That makes sense," he said. "When you explain it like that, Tom, I can understand what you mean. I see now why you didn't want to eat any of the cookies. Why didn't you explain it like that yesterday?"

"I . . . I guess I was afraid, Eric. But I did eat one of the cookies and that was wrong. I'm going to see Mr. Frost and ask him to forgive me."

"You're going to do what?" interrupted Eric. "You must be crazy. Why would you apologize to him? I'm the one who stole the cookies."

"Because I was part of it, that's why. I won't feel right until they're paid for, Eric. I'm going to pay for them."

"You are sure different, Tom," said Eric through a half smile. "I've never seen a guy like you. To show you I'm not really THAT bad, I'll go with you to see Old Man Frost."

The storekeeper accepted the boys' apologies and received payment for the stolen goods. Even though he didn't say so, Eric felt better inside. When the two arrived back home, Eric asked Tom if they could talk some more. They spent nearly an hour chatting in the Stenner's front yard.

"I just want to tell you, Tom, that your religion kind of rubbed off on me today. It takes a lot of courage to do what you did."

"It really isn't me, Eric," replied Tom. "It's God who lives in me. He helps me everyday. There's a lot about Him that I would like to share with you, I . . . I . . . mean if you want to hear about Him."

"It's all right with me as long as you're doing the talking, Tom. I don't know anything about that stuff."

Eric hesitated and then continued. "By the way, I'll bring the money for the cookies over tonight. I'm the one who should pay for them, not you."

That night Tom told his parents what had taken place during the day. Their faces beamed with joy when he shared with them the good news that Eric was going to both Sunday School and church with him on Sunday.

"And to think," he said, smiling, "it all started over that one cookie." Tom Upland felt good inside. His heart was now right with the Lord and Eric would be in church with him on Sunday.

26

His
Way
is
Best

The light in Amy's room was spotted immediately by her father. Bob Stoner wiped the tears from his eyes as he looked up at Room 602 of the city's General Hospital. Behind that window lay one of the most precious possessions he would ever have on earth—his seven-year-old daughter, Amy.

It all seemed like a dream to the young father. Six months earlier Bob and Amy had stood by the graveside of Evelyn Stoner. The 27 year-old mother and wife had been struck by a hit-and-run driver in front of the Stoner residence. Evelyn's favorite hymn was sung before her body was lowered into the grave. Little Amy had heard the words so many times from her mother's lips that she knew them by heart. She sung out lustily as she clung tightly to her daddy's hand.

"Blessed assurance, Jesus is mine. Oh, what a foretaste of glory divine.
Heir of salvation, purchased of God; born of His Spirit, washed in His Blood."

Pastor Hay looked down at the little girl and smiled. Her voice could be heard above the others at the graveside.

The lump in Bob's throat would not allow him to sing. The sudden death of his wife, the scene at the open grave, little Amy's voice—all was almost too much for him to bear.

"Lord," he prayed, "I know Your strength is sufficient. Thank You for Your faithfulness."

Bob Stoner and his only child did well as they adjusted to life without a wife and mother in the home. There were moments when the crushing grief would return, but Bob always found the Lord to be his strength.

Nearly three months after the funeral Amy complained to her father about the pain in her throat. "I wanted to tell you before, Daddy, but I didn't want you to worry," said the pretty little girl. "It will go away when you give me medicine."

Since the family doctor had been a close friend to the Stoners for years, attending the same church, Bob gave him an immediate call.

"Ted, this is Bob Stoner. I'm sorry to bother you at this time of night, but Amy seems to have a bad infection in her throat." The concerned father explained to Ted Andrews how Amy had told him about the pain in her throat during the evening meal. "She says it has been hurting her for the past week, but she didn't tell me because she didn't want me to worry."

"I'll be right over, Bob," answered the doctor.

The physician's examination of Amy's throat revealed a far worse condition than he thought he would find. "I want to run some tests tomorrow morning at the hospital. Can you have Amy there at eight o'clock, Bob?"

"Whatever you say, Ted," answered the young father, sensing a real concern on the part of the doctor.

The next morning Amy was put to sleep so the doctor could perform a thorough examination on her throat. By mid-morning Dr. Andrews was with Bob in a consultation room. He reached out and placed his hand on Bob's shoulder.

"It's serious, Bob. Amy has cancer. It's a wonder she can even speak."

Bob felt a prickly sensation run through his body. He opened his mouth to speak but couldn't. Tears filled his eyes. Finally he spoke.

"She's all I have, Ted. Amy is all I have in this world."

"Bob," comforted his friend, "for some reason God is allowing this to happen in your life and He is in control. I know it is easy for me to talk. Janice and I have not experienced anything as you have, but I do know that God loves you and He loves Amy. He is not going to allow anything to happen except it be for your good and His glory."

"I know that, Ted," responded the grieving father. "I'm not doubting God, but it still hurts. I felt that my heart had been torn from my body when Evelyn was suddenly taken from me and now my only child, our little Amy, has cancer. I just don't understand it, Ted. Someday I know I will, but right now I don't."

As Bob reached the entrance of the hospital, he was greeted by one of the nurses who was leaving. "Good evening, Mr. Stoner. How are you tonight?"

"I'm fine, thank you," responded Bob, with a smile. Everyone was so kind. Amy was loved by all who saw her and especially since they knew she would not be alive much longer.

The elevator door opened on the sixth floor and the anxious father stepped out into the familiar hallway. He opened the door to Amy's room and found Dr. Andrews and two nurses by her bed.

"Amy, here's your daddy," said the doctor, motioning toward Bob. "I'll see you later, Bob," he whispered and the nurses left the room.

The young father leaned over the bed and looked into the face of his precious little girl. "I love you, Amy," he whispered. "I love you, Honey." The cancer had advanced to the point that Amy could no longer speak. Tubes were everywhere, protruding from the tiny body. Bob fought back the tears.

"Jesus loves you, Honey. Do you want Daddy to sing?" Amy's eyes answered for her. Bob began singing softly.

"Jesus loves me, this I know, for the Bible tells me so.
Little ones to Him belong. They are weak, but He is strong.
Yes, Jesus loves me. Yes, Jesus loves me. Yes, Jesus loves me.
The Bible tells me so."

The look on Amy's face and the movement in her eyes indicated she was trying to say something.

"Do you want daddy to sing some more, Honey?" Again the answer was positive. "How about Blessed Assurance?" Bob noticed a flicker of light in the big brown eyes. Slowly and softly he sang.

"Blessed assurance, Jesus is mine. Oh, what a foretaste of glory divine.
Heir of salvation, purchased of God; born of his Spirit, washed in His Blood.
This is my story, this is my song; praising my Savior all the day long.
This is my story, this is my song; praising my Savior all the day long."

When he finished singing, the heavy-hearted father detected a slight smile on his daughter's face. Before he left the room that night, Amy was asleep. Ted Andrews met Bob in the hallway as he came out of Amy's room.

"Amy will soon be with the Lord, Bob. There's nothing more we can do for her."

That night Bob Stoner knelt in his room and asked God to take Amy home. Whatever You want for me, Lord, that's what I want, too. I still don't understand why all of this has happened; first Evelyn and now Amy. But I know this is no mistake. I accept Your perfect will."

As he lay in the darkness, Bob sensed God's perfect peace. He knew that within a very short time, Amy would be with the Lord.

"Not my will, Lord, but Thine be done," said Bob as he drifted off to sleep. He could not know that in three days he would be standing with Pastor Hay beside a tiny grave, once again singing, "Blessed Assurance, Jesus is Mine."

27
God's
Appointments
(Based on a true story)

"Jesus died for you, Bill. He paid the penalty for your sins."
Cathy leafed through her Bible for still another verse to read to
her friend, Bill Scott. Lunch hour was almost over and Cathy still
had not touched the sandwich in the brown paper bag beside her.
Witnessing was more important to her than eating and especially
since Bill was so close to accepting Christ as his Savior.

"I really believe He died for me, Cathy," answered Bill. "I can see
what you are telling me."

"Then why not accept Him now?" continued Cathy. "Would you
like me to pray with you, right here?"

The tall handsome, college student bowed his head and there,
seated on the parking lot bench, prayed, asking God to forgive him
of his sins and save him. Cathy looked at her watch.

"Hey, it's time to get back to work. We'll be late if we don't hurry."

"But . . . but, your lunch," said Bill, nodding at the untouched
paper bag.

"Oh, I can do without that," laughed Cathy. "Talking with you
about Jesus was far more important than eating."

Cathy saw a big difference in Bill Scott's life in the store where
they both worked. She noticed that he wasn't drinking any more
and he was filled with questions about the Bible and his new faith.
She bought a Bible the day after he was saved and gave it to him.
She also invited him to church and made it a point to introduce him
to the young adults' Sunday School class.

Two weeks after Bill was led to the Lord, he asked Cathy to go to a baseball game with him.

"I would love to have you go with me, Cathy. I had wanted to ask you out for several months before I got saved, but I knew that you wouldn't go with me to the places where I was used to going."

Bill looked away as he spoke the next words.

"You're a very special girl, Cathy. I knew you were different from the other girls from the first time I met you."

The relationship between Bill and Cathy was a blessing to those who were close to them. The weeks and months rapidly passed. A year after their first date, Cathy accepted an engagement ring from Bill. The church family was delighted when the wedding date was set for the following summer. The happy couple knew that God had brought them together. They committed themselves to Him for whatever He had planned for them.

June the nineteenth was an exciting day for Bill and Cathy. As the tall groom watched his bride walk down the aisle of the small church, he recalled once again how God had used her to introduce him to the Savior.

"Thank You, dear Father, for Cathy. Thank You for bringing her into my life."

Together, the young married couple worked in their church. Bill had grown tremendously in the things of the Lord. They not only directed the youth work, but each taught Sunday School classes as well.

The Lord blessed the Scotts in their second year of marriage with a baby boy. Cathy was sure the baby would be Ruth Ann, but was perfectly happy when little William Paul made his appearance.

"He's beautiful, Bill," she said, holding her baby for the first time.

"And he has black hair like me," laughed the father, teasingly making a face at Cathy.

Little William, Jr., brought an even greater joy to the young couple.

"I never realized life could be so wonderful," said Bill, as he stood by the baby's crib the day he came home from the hospital. "We have much for which to be thankful."

Laughter filled the Scott's home as the parents enjoyed their new baby. The weeks seemed to fly by with little William showing development with each new day. It was seven months after his birth when they heard the disturbing news. Cathy had gone to the doctor for a checkup and was told that he wanted to run some tests on her in the hospital. The test results were positive and exploratory surgery was scheduled.

Bill sat in deep thought in the hospital waiting room. Cathy's mother had arrived by plane the day before and was caring for the baby.

"Father," prayed Bill, "she belongs to You. We both want Your will to be done." Tears coursed down the young husband's face as he prayed.

An hour after Cathy was taken into the operating room, the surgeon appeared in the waiting room and asked Bill to go with him to his office. His heart beat hard as he listened.

"Only a miracle of the Lord will save Cathy, Bill." The Christian physician put his arm around Bill's shoulder. "I don't know why we haven't had any signs before this. The cancer has already spread to several organs."

"How long does she have to live, Doctor?" questioned the grieving husband.

"Maybe two months, Bill. Possibly three at the most," responded the doctor.

Bill buried his face in his hands and sobbed.

"Excuse me, Dr. White, but I just can't help it. She means so much to me."

Cathy was informed of her condition two days after surgery. Bill was sitting beside her bed when Dr. White explained what he had found. The young mother listened intently to every word. Bill marveled at the way she took the news. Before Dr. White left Bill and Cathy alone, he prayed with them.

"He's a wonderful doctor, Bill," said Cathy as the door closed behind the physician.

"He sure is," added the Bill. "Thank the Lord for a doctor who knows and loves Him."

"Honey," said Cathy, reaching out to take Bill's hand, "I want to tell you how I feel about what is happening to us." Her pretty face reflected the Lord's peace.

"God loves us very much, Bill. He loves you and William and me and wants His best for all of us. I know I'm going to be with Him soon. Because He does love me, He's allowing me to fulfill His will by taking me home to be with Him. You will follow, Honey, but only in His time." Cathy squeezed Bill's hand and then continued.

"It's only natural for this separation to hurt, but it's what He wants, Bill." Again Cathy hesitated. "I want that, too, Honey," she whispered.

"I really do."

The funeral service was attended by several hundred people. Mixed feelings were reflected by nearly all. Testimonies of praise were given for Cathy's victorious life. Many cried as they watched Bill beside the open grave with little William in his arms.

"Face to Face with Christ my Saviour," one of Cathy's favorite hymns, was sung. It was a long trip for Bill as he drove back home with Cathy's parents and William.

The next three years were lonely years for Bill. Several mothers at the church offered their services to babysit William while Bill worked. One of them was a young widow whose husband had died about the same time as Cathy. She and Bill had often shared in short conversations when he picked up William after work. The more Bill saw Penny and prayed for her, the more he seemed to like her and wanted to be around her.

It was difficult for Bill when he asked her to go for a walk one day. He noticed the twinkle in her eyes as she responded to his request.

"Why, Bill Scott, I thought you'd never ask me!" They both laughed at her remark. Somehow Bill felt in his heart that Penny Evans would someday be Mrs. Penny Scott.

Bill and Penny's courtship was welcomed by their friends.

"It's about time he noticed you," said one of the older ladies from the church to Penny one day in the grocery store.

Twelve months after their engagement, Penny became Mrs. William Scott. The happy couple became a family of five with the addition of Penny's two children and William, Jr.

As they were sitting in the den one evening, Penny surprised Bill by mentioning Bible school.

"I know we've not talked about this, Bill, but since I've been saved, I've wondered if the Lord would ever call me into full-time service.
"I, too, have often thought about serving the Lord in a full-time
Bill looked up at Penny. He knew she was serious.

"It's not a coincidence that you mention that, Honey," said Bill. "I, too, have often thought about serving the Lord in a full time ministry. Cathy loved the Lord and was a wonderful wife and mother but she always said she knew she wasn't cut out for the ministry."

A week later, Bill and Penny invited Pastor and Mrs. Taylor over to share with them their thoughts about Bible school.

"Penny and I have been praying about going to Bible school,

Pastor," said Bill. "In fact, we both have thought about such a possibility for years."

"That doesn't surprise me at all, Bill," responded the pleasant-looking pastor. "I, too, have thought from almost the time you were saved that you were material for the ministry."

That night the two couples prayed together as Bill and Penny committed their lives to the Lord for full-time service. The following Sunday morning the young husband and wife, along with their three children, walked forward to make known their decision.

"This is one of the happiest days of our lives," spoke Bill to the church family. "As you all know, both Penny and I have experienced difficult times in the past, but the Lord saw us through them. Bible school will be another step in fulfilling the Lord's will for us."

Bill waited a moment before he continued. Tears appeared in his eyes.

"Our disappointments became God's appointments. We thank Him for all He has done for us."

"Amen," whispered Penny, squeezing Bill's hand.

28

Tracks
in the
Snow

"When and where did you last see your little girl, Mrs. Sands?" The concerned policeman reached out and patted the young mother on her shoulder. He felt her body tremble with the agonizing grief that had gripped her.

Sylvia Sands sobbed as she responded to the officer's question. "It was right after lunch. She went out to the back yard to play with Muffin, our miniature poodle. I called out to Becky about 30 minutes later and she and Muffin were both gone."

"About what time was that?" asked the policeman.

"I think it was about one o'clock. Yes, it was one o'clock because the mailman was just coming up the front walk when I checked to see if Becky had gone out on the street. She never has and, too, we have a fence around the back yard."

Sylvia had been a widow for five months. Her husband, Jim, was fatally injured when he fell from the third floor of a building where he was a construction worker. A month after he had died, Sylvia gave birth to a seven-pound boy. She named him James Walter Sands, Jr., after his father.

Baby James laid sleeping nearby in his crib. The worried mother glanced over at him now and then as she spoke. She held in her trembling hands a recent picture of Becky which the police wanted for identification purposes. While they were talking, Sylvia noticed that a light snow had begun to fall. This brought an even greater look of concern on her face.

The doorbell interrupted the conversation between Sylvia and the policeman. Hurrying to the door, she saw it was Pastor and Mrs. Pletcher.

"Hello, Sylvia," spoke the pleasant looking man. "We came over as soon as we heard about Becky. Is there any news yet?"

"Nothing yet, Pastor. Please come in," said Sylvia, closing the door behind them. "Pastor and Mrs. Pletcher, this is Lieutenant Cobb. He came to get some information on Becky."

Tears rolled down Sylvia's cheeks as she spoke. "Please excuse me," she said softly. "I just can't help myself." Mrs. Pletcher put her arms around the distraught mother.

Soon the lieutenant was ready to leave. He assured Sylvia he would do all he could to find Becky and that they would be in touch with her to let her know of the search operations. Before he left, Sylvia mentioned to him that Muffin had only three legs.

"We almost had her put to sleep when she lost her leg in the snow blower last winter, but Becky's pleas persuaded us to keep her." A slight smile appeared on Sylvia's face when she mentioned this.

After the officer had gone, Pastor and Mrs. Pletcher visited and then had a time of prayer. As the pastor was praying, sounds of footsteps came from the front porch. Sylvia opened the door and discovered one of the men from down the street.

"Hello, Mr. Engle," greeted Sylvia.

"Hello, Mrs. Sands," spoke the middle-aged man, seemingly out of breath. "Word about your little Becky got around really fast and we neighbors have been searching the area. We found Muffin's tracks in the snow. Her three legs gave her away. I left the group and ran to tell you. The others continued to follow her tracks."

"I'll stay with the baby, Sylvia, if you and pastor want to go with Mr. Engle," offered Mrs. Pletcher.

The excited mother hurriedly put on her coat and was rushing across the yard beside the pastor and Mr. Engle when, two houses away, they saw some neighbors coming with Becky. Muffin was darting in and out between their feet.

"Becky!" called Sylvia, running toward her little girl, "Honey, are you all right?"

"I'm all right, Mommy," replied Becky, throwing her arms around her mother's neck. "I was so scared."

The relieved group of neighbors entered the Sands' house. Pastor Pletcher called the police station to inform them that Becky had been found. Little James, awakened from his sleep, began to cry and was quickly picked up by one of the visitors.

Half crying, Becky told her mother what had happened. "Muffin ran after a cat. I tried to stop her but she wouldn't listen. The gate was open and she ran right out." The little girl stopped long enough to shake a scolding finger at the small, gray poodle. Several in the group laughed.

Becky continued. "The cat ran into a garage way down by the corner. Muffin ran into the garage after it. I couldn't find them when I got there."

"There are two rooms in the back of my garage," said Mrs. Johnson, the owner of the garage. "Evidently the cat and dog ran in and came out without Becky seeing them. She thought they were in one of the rooms. I came out and closed the door. I didn't see anyone in the garage. Then I went shopping with a friend of mine who lives on the West side."

"You poor dear," said Sylvia, hugging Becky close to her.

"I called for you, Mommy, but no one came. I was cold, too." Becky cuddled close to her mother.

"It was Mr. Engle who spotted the dog's tracks in your back yard," spoke one of the men. "He called our attention to the fact that the tracks were made by a three-legged dog. We followed her tracks to the garage and there we heard Becky's voice."

"Thank you, Muffin," said Sylvia, patting the family pet on her head. "You were the Lord's answer to our prayers."

The entire group bowed their heads as Pastor Pletcher prayed, thanking God for bringing Becky safely back home.

That night before she went to sleep, Becky prayed with her mother. "Thank You, Jesus, for helping Muffin to help the people find me."

The little three-legged poodle lying quietly beside the bed perked up an ear when she heard her name.

(Reprinted by permission of REgular Baptist Press)

29

Safe
at
Home

"There's a high drive into left!" shouted the announcer. "It's going . . . going . . . It's gone! Another home run for Tim Long!"

Frank Hart stood up and slapped his hands together. "Great game! Those Bull Dogs have really come to life all of a sudden. And that Tim Long, why he's hitting the pitches like he owns them."

"You're right, Frank," said his father who was listening to the play-off game with his son. "If they win one more, they'll take the State Championship. I'm sure glad they are broadcasting the games this year."

Andrew Hart loved baseball. Even though he was middle-aged, he enjoyed playing in pick-up neighborhood ball games in the nearby park. He had played semi-professional baseball in his younger days and at one time even had a tryout with the St. Louis Cardinals system.

"By the way, Frank," asked his father, "how is Tim since he made his decision to accept Christ?" Andrew was referring to the recent evangelistic meetings at their church. Coach Johnson, a deacon in the church, had invited his team to the services one night. At the close of the service, Tim went forward and made a public profession of Christ.

"His life has really changed, Dad," answered Frank. "Would you believe the other day he bowed his head in the cafeteria to thank the Lord for his food? One of the guys asked him if he felt sick. There's nothing fake about Tim. He's a real Christian."

The following Sunday as they came out of church, Frank and Tim were talking about the championship playoff games and the victorious Bull Dogs.

"You know, Frank," said Tim with a serious look on his face, "I'd love to play professional baseball and there's nothing wrong with that, but I have a strange feeling inside me that there's something else for me. I don't quite understand what it is, but I know it's there."

Frank knew that Tim had been offered a scholarship to play college ball and could possibly go on from there to a professional career.

"Well, all I can say, Tim, is to pray about it." Frank smiled at his friend. "I'll pray with you."

As the two young men parted to go home, Frank could hardly believe the spiritual growth in his friend. He smiled thinking of the small Testament that was showing in Tim's shirt pocket. Frank had never seen any new Christian grow so fast in the things of the Lord.

That same night in church when the pastor gave time for testimonies, Tim was the first one to speak. He told of their recent play-off games and how he had the opportunity to witness to a number of players on the other teams. The church family sat with hearts filled with joy as they listened to the new Christian.

"I have a big burden on my heart that I want to share with you," said Tim. He cleared his throat and continued. Tim sounded like he was near tears.

"My Mom and Dad are lost and need Christ. I have witnessed to them, but they refuse to believe in my Savior." The tall high school senior stopped and then went on. "Please pray for them as well as my brother, Jim. Thank you dear friends."

There was hardly a dry eye in the congregation when Tim finished. Few had ever made such an impact on the church family.

The next day, Frank and Tim were playing a game with a pickup neighborhood team. One of the players noticed that Tim began to stagger. Before he could reach Tim, the tall first baseman fell heavily to the ground. Andrew Hart watching the game from the bench, rushed to the stricken player whose muscular form was stretched out on the soft, green grass.

"Are you alright, Tim?" he asked with a worried look on his face.

"I'm all right, Mr. Hart," responded Tim, blinking his eyes. "I don't know what happened. I just felt myself falling and the next thing I knew, you were kneeling beside me."

The neighborhood hero was soon on his feet and continued playing even though Frank and his father asked him to call it a day.

"I've promised these kids for the last two weeks that I'd play ball with them today," said Tim with his ever pleasant look. "I can't let them down."

The next several days were days of concern for Tim Long. He fainted five more times and in the last fall, struck his head on the corner of a table, leaving a deep gash in his forehead. Andrew Hart was available to take him to the doctor.

"I'm admitting you to the hospital, Tim," Doctor Brown said as he finished the last of twelve stitches. "I want to run some tests on you to determine the cause of these blackouts."

"O.K.," Tim said slowly, "but remember, I promised the kids that I'd play a game with them this Saturday."

The middle-aged doctor smiled. "I'll put a 'rush' on all your papers." The doctor gave Tim a pat on his shoulder.

Two days later, Dr. Brown stood in the living room of the Long home. His face showed strain. As the high school team physician, he knew Tim well.

"I'm sorry, Phil and Bertha, to have to give you this news." The family doctor had just told Tim's parents that the tests revealed a brain tumor.

Bertha Long gripped her husband's hand tightly. Her eyes filled with tears as she waited for the doctor's next statement.

"I'm requesting permission for immediate surgery. It's the only thing we can do."

"You have our permission, Dr. Brown," spoke Tim's father. "Does Tim know anything about this report?"

"No, he doesn't," answered the sympathetic doctor. "If you want me to tell him, I will do it. You know, Tim and I are pretty close friends."

Later in the hospital room, Tim listened intently to Dr. Brown's report. "So, that's it, Tim. I would like to have surgery done immediately."

Tim reached over and picked up his Bible from his bedside table. "You know, Dr. Brown, many young men my age would be frightened and possibly even angry in hearing such news. But I know that my Heavenly Father orders my steps. He knows all about my stops and goes."

The family physician continued to be amazed in the new Tim Long. He marvelled in the courage demonstrated by the young athlete.

Two days later, Frank Hart sat with Phil and Bertha Long in the hospital waiting room. The moment Dr. Brown appeared in the open door way, they knew something was wrong. Tim's father stood up to meet the approaching doctor.

"Would you all come to my office, please?" he asked nodding his head toward a nearby room. Frank and the anxious parents followed the green clad doctor into the small room.

"It doesn't look good," said Dr. Brown. "The operation confirmed our diagnosis. Tim has a tumor which is not operable. We will treat it, but I don't give you much hope."

The three stood in silence as the news made its impact on their already heavy hearts.

Three days later, Phil and Bertha Long sat beside Tim's bed. He was conscious but was failing steadily.

"Mom and Dad," spoke Tim hesitantly, "I know there's no hope for me, humanly speaking. My life belongs to the Lord and whatever He wants is all right with me."

Tim's mother turned her head as the tears trickled down her face. She listened attentively as her son continued. "I'll soon be with the Lord. I'm not afraid of death. For me to die is gain. It's wonderful to know that I'll spend eternity with the One I love." He reached over and took his mother's hand.

"More than anything else in the world, I wish you both knew Jesus as your Savior. Won't you accept Him?" Tim paused as though he was waiting for an answer. "You both know how He changed my life."

Tim's parents looked at each other. Never had they felt so much in need of the Lord. Tim's mother patted him on the arm.

"You're so very right, Tim. I really do need Him. Dad and I both need Him to do for us what He has done for you."

Within the minute, Phil and Bertha Long knelt beside their son's bed and asked God to forgive their sins and to save them. Tim's face beamed with joy as he witnessed the wonderful event.

The next two days seemed to drag by. Thursday afternoon found Phil and Bertha along side the familiar hospital bed. The doctor had just confirmed that Tim was dead. Their hearts were crushed as they turned to leave the room. The sheet-draped body lying on the bed was a grim reminder of death, but yet, deep within them was the precious hope that they would see their son again.

Bertha turned her tear-stained face to her husband. "I can't explain it, Phil," she said, wiping her eyes, "but I believe that in his death, Tim did as much as many of us will do in a lifetime for God."

"You're right, Honey," answered her heart-broken husband. "I know that God used our Tim to turn our lives around."

"Yes," responded Bertha, "and we'll never be the same because of Tim's life—and death."

30
Not
In
Vain

"**P**lease be careful, Samuel," spoke the worried mother. "If you see any of the rebels, go to the forest immediately and hide there."

The Branza family was known for its testimony for the Lord in the village of Kota-Jo. The nearly 1200 residents knew that Tako Branza and his wife Kolo were not only faithful in their attendance in the local church but that their children, too, were dedicated Christians.

"I'll be careful, Mama," called ten year old Samuel as he left the privacy of the grass mat fence which circled the family dwelling.

Only two days before, a band of rebels came into the village and looted and burned several of the small African shops. Since the children's class was held on the nearby mission station, Kolo thought that her son would be safe there. She stood in the open doorway of the dried mud block house and watched Samuel until he finally disappeared behind some tall elephant grass. Several other children joined him on their way to class.

"Father," the concerned mother prayed, "I commit my family to You. Use us for Your glory. Help us not to compromise Your testimony for the sake of safety."

Kolo thought of her husband and the two older children working in their cotton garden some two miles away. How easy it would be for any of the rebel bands to hurt them or even take their lives if they so desired. The middle-aged mother carried her heavy wood mortar outside to beat some grain for their evening meal. Surely the entire family would be ready for a delicious meal of their favorite food when they came home—cooked grain mush and fish sauce.

"Hello, Kolo," called the lady next door. "Can I bring you anything from the store? I plan to return right away."

Kolo remembered that they used the last of their kerosene the night before and hurried into the house for the empty liter bottle. In a moment she returned handing the bottle and some money to her friend.

"Thank you, Keke," said Kolo smiling. The morning sun caught the raised facial tribal scars sending tiny shadows across her face. "I'm glad the shipment of kerosene arrived after the rebel attack. They would have burned that too."

The two women exchanged handshakes and Kolo began pounding the grain—her thoughts on her family.

Missionary Mary Taber closed the screen door of her little brick cottage and started down the path to the mission station chapel. She glanced over her shoulder to make sure the screen door was completely closed. It was only the week before that it was left ajar in her haste to get to class, and upon her return home, she found a seven foot spitting cobra in her dining room. Several children saw her and ran to walk with her.

"What is our lesson today, Miss Mary?" asked one of the girls. "Is it about Daniel in the lions' den?"

"I know," spoke another. "It's about Joseph and the pit."

Mary smiled. "You're both wrong. I have a surprise story for you today."

The children laughed at their teacher's remark. They knew that whatever it would be, it would be a good story. They loved to hear Miss Mary tell them stories from the Bible.

Class began by taking roll call. The children seemed a bit more excited than usual. Mary noticed Samuel sitting in the front row. "Samuel," she said softly, "would you please begin our class today with prayer?"

Samuel was pleased that he was asked to pray. "Thank you, Lord, for our teacher, Miss Taber. Help her as she teaches from your Book."

Mary was in the middle of her story when she heard the shouting. Looking up, she saw several men entering the back of the chapel. They had guns in their hands.

"What's going on here?" one of the men shouted. He turned to Mary who stood still, hoping the children would follow her example.

"What are you teaching these children?" he demanded. "You're a foreign devil, woman. You don't belong here. This is our country."

One of the boys beside Samuel jumped to his feet and tried to run out of the chapel. He was immediately struck down by a rifle butt.

"Please don't hurt them!" cried Mary. "They can't do you any harm."

Uncontrollable fear gripped the class. Many cried out for help. The rebels turned to beat the children. Some of them started for the door dragging boys and girls behind them. Mary tried to calm the children so they would not anger the rebels any more than they were. The screams of one little girl was silenced by a loud blast from a rifle. Mary looked through the back door to see Samuel bending over a friend to help him. Another shot burst forth sending the ten year old sprawling on top of the body under him. The spreading red blotch on Samuel's shirt told the grim story.

Kolo stiffened with fear when she heard the gun shot. She dropped her pounding pole and headed for the mission station as fast as her legs would take her. Other villagers joined with her, some of whom were already crying the death wail. By the time the villagers reached the station, the rebels had left leaving behind them five dead—three boys and two girls.

Mary was on her knees beside the body of one of the girls. She lifted her tear-stained face to watch the approaching villagers.

"Miss Mary!" called Kolo. "Have you seen Samuel? Is he all right?"

The missionary teacher rose to her feet and put her arms around her African sister. "Kolo," said Mary weeping, "your Samuel is home with the Lord. He was shot while trying to help one of his friends."

Kolo sunk to her knees and buried her face in her hands. Her body shook with sobs as she gazed upon the cloth-draped body of her youngest child.

"Father," she prayed aloud, "I know you don't make any mistakes. For some reason you've allowed this to happen and have taken our Samuel home to heaven."

As Kolo prayed, Mary knelt beside her, putting her arm around the grieving mother.

"Thank you, Father, that we don't have to sorrow as those who don't believe in Jesus. Help Tako and the boys as they hear this news. Please save the souls of those men who committed this terrible crime today."

Kolo was helped to her feet by several friends. A runner was dispatched to the gardens with the news of the attack.

That evening, a great number of people gathered in the village of Kota-Jo. Instead of the dancing and wailing related with the death of unbelievers, hymns were sung and testimonies given. Mary sat beside Kolo. Toward midnight, Tako raised his hand to get the attention of everyone.

"My friends, it is late and I know you are tired. We will bury our children tomorrow and I want you to get some sleep."

The clicking of tongues could be heard, indicating agreement with what Tako was saying.

"I do want to say something to you before you go to your beds. This is no coincidence that we are meeting like this tonight. It is not a mistake that lying here before us are five small lifeless bodies of those we loved."

Tako fought back the tears as he spoke. He put his hand to his face to hide his emotions.

"These children are dead physically but alive spiritually." He pointed to the bodies while he spoke.

"There are some of you sitting here who are alive physically but dead spiritually. If Samuel could speak, he would ask you to see yourselves as lost sinners and accept God's sacrifice for your sins— His Son, Jesus."

Many bowed their heads as Tako spoke. "I'm no preacher and I don't pretend to be one." A few laughed at his remark.

"I can tell you, however, that Jesus died for you. If you confess your sins and receive Him into your hearts, He will forgive you of your sins and give you everlasting life. That's what all of these children did. Samuel received Jesus one day in Miss Mary's class. He's in heaven now."

As he spoke, several men and women stood up, indicating they wanted to receive Christ as Saviour.

"Thank the Lord," continued Tako. "Through their death, our little ones have been instrumental in bring some of you to accept Jesus. You see, dear friends, their deaths are not in vain."

The soft clicking of tongues could be heard among the Africans. God was at work in their midst.

31
Doli's
Sacrifice

News of the recent raid by guerrilla bands on nearby villages struck fear into the hearts of the people of Ngou. The latest raid was only two miles away in which half the houses in the village were burned and eight people, including the chief, were killed.

Six years had passed since Pastor Moses and his wife Doli went to Ngou to establish a church in the small village. It was a difficult work to begin because of the tremendous influence of the area witch-doctor. Once the little work was established, however, excitement grew as pastor and people reached out to the neighboring villages with the Gospel. One of these villages was Biobe.

"My heart aches for those dear people," said Doli, speaking of the victims of the last raid, "and to think that we were making such good progress with Chief Sousou. I don't think he has missed a church service for the past two months."

Moses looked up from where he was preparing some sermon notes at a small folding table. "He may have made a decision to accept Christ without our knowing it. There has been a lot of personal witnessing going on in that village. Since the chief's assistant was saved, I know of three people who were led to the Lord by him."

The tall Sara tribesman stood to his feet and walked slowly to the open door of the large dried mud block house. A troubled look was on his face as he gazed out across the village. "I must try and get to Biobe," spoke Moses. "I know the forests are alive with rebel bands but those people need me." He clapped his hands lightly to indicate that he had a plan.

Doli got up and walked over beside her husband. "What are you thinking of doing, Moses?" her voice reflecting a deep concern.

His brown eyes showing his determination, Moses turned and looked at his wife. "I'm going to go there tonight after dark. I know the forests well and I don't think anyone will see me."

The villagers at Biobe were stunned by the devastating raid on their village. Some thirty houses were burned. The eight mounds of dirt in the center of the village were a grim reminder of not only the terrible tragedy that took place but also of the ever-lurking danger of a repeat attack.

Two days had passed since the raid took place and no outsiders made any attempt to reach Biobe. Everyone greatly feared for his life.

Moses waited about two hours after the sun went down before he began to get ready for his dangerous walk through the jungle to go to Biobe. He chose the darkest clothing he owned for the hike. If he would be discovered by any of the rebels, he knew it was certain death and probably without any questions asked.

He peered out through a small window to see if any of the villagers were still outside their huts. It was best that no one see him leave. Feeling certain that there was no one near his house, Moses quietly slipped out the door and vanished into the nearby forest. Once inside the cover of the trees, he found a familiar path which headed in the direction of Biobe.

Every few minutes, Moses would stop to listen. Even though the many night sounds of the forest were familiar to him, he was startled when a large bat flapped its way out of a nearby tree. The village pastor was well aware of the awesome fact that he could meet death any moment.

An inward feeling caused Moses to stop abruptly. He stood perfectly still straining his eyes and ears to pick up something. There was someone talking off to his right. He could not hear their words but only the muffled sound fo their voice.

"Who could it be?" Moses whispered to himself.

He tiptoed slowly toward the sound of the voice. The closer he came, the more he realized that there was only one voice and it sounded like someone in pain. He was now only yards away.

"I. . .need. . .help," came the voice again. "Somebody. . . help. . .me."

Moses recognized the voice. It was Tago, the chief's assistant at Biobe. The pastor was quickly beside the man lying on the ground.

"Tago," spoke Moses quietly. "It's me, Pastor Moses. Where are you hurt?"

The wounded African raised his hand and pointed to his right leg. "I . . . got . . . shot . . . in . . . the . . . leg," he mumbled.

"Don't talk anymore, Tago," said Moses, as he unfastened a flat water canteen from his belt. He carefully place the canteen to Tago's mouth. "Just sip a little at a time."

The water seemed to bring strength to the hurt African. "I tried . . . to . . . reach . . . your village," he spoke hesitantly. "I was hit . . . just as I . . . reached the grass. I have laid . . . here for two days . . . afraid to go on. I didn't want . . . to leave a trail . . . of my blood for them . . . to follow."

The best he could, Moses washed the bullet wound. He took his undershirt off and tied it around Tago's leg.

"I thank God . . . you came . . . Pastor," said Tago. "But you are in danger. The forest . . . is filled with . . . rebels."

"Don't talk anymore, Tago. Save your strength. You will need it."

Moses sat beside his friend and told him in a whisper that he was on his way to Biobe to see if he could be of any help. "Right after the raid, one of the men from the village came to Ngou and told us what had taken place. I wanted to come immediately but I didn't think it was wise. Then, too, I may not have found you, Tago."

Within the hour, Moses was on his way back to Ngou carrying his precious cargo on his back. Every fifty yards or so he stopped to rest. Three more stops and he would be close enough to see the village. He thought how surprised Doli would be to see him and Tago.

He was about to pick up Tago when he heard gun shots and shouting. "Oh, no!" he cried out, "they're attacking Ngou and Doli's alone!"

Moses quickly unfastened the canteen of water and gave it to Tago. "Crawl in the bushes over there, Tago. That's a good place to hide. I'll be back later."

Without another word, the concerned pastor was off running towards his village. The flames from the burning huts leaped high, lighting the entire village. The terrified African ran straight to his house only to find that the flaming grass and bamboo roof had fallen into the building. Anything that could burn was ablaze. He shielded his face with his hands and moved as close as he could to the burning house.

"Doli! Can you hear me?" shouted Moses. "Doli! Are you in

there?"

"She's in there, Pastor," spoke a teenage girl. "I was in our house looking out the window and saw what happened."

Moses cupped his face in his hands and wept. One of the men of the village came over to him and put his arm around the sorrowing husband.

"What did you see, Ann?" asked Moses. "Tell me all that you saw."

The young lady, who was in Doli's girls' class, wept as she spoke. "When the shooting started, I ran to the window and looked out. Some of the rebels were at your house banging on the door. They finally broke the door open and went inside. They came out dragging Mrs. Doli by her arm."

"Oh, Pastor," the girl sobbed, "it was terrible."

"I know, Ann," said Moses, "but I must hear what happened."

Ann continued, "They kept shouting at her, asking where they could find you. When she didn't answer, one of the men shot her. She fell to the ground but slowly got to her feet. Even though she was hurt, she was able to break loose and run back into the house. They then set fire to the roof. . .and. . .then you came."

"Dear Doli," cried Moses, wiping the tears from his face, "She died trying to protect me. Now, she's with the Lord whom she loved so much."

The death wail of the villagers suddenly brought Moses back to the whole tragedy that was taking place. The light from the burning houses showed several villagers lying motionless on the ground. Overwhelmed in grief, the faithful pastor started walking to the nearest victim.

"Doli is now with you, Father," he prayed as he approached a group of wailing villagers surrounding a body on the ground. "Help me to minister to my people in this terrible time."

An hour later, Moses headed back to the forest to get Tago. One of the Christian families invited the pastor and Tago to stay with them.

It was nearly morning when Moses finally fell asleep. Before he did, however, he thanked God for a wonderful wife who was willing to die rather than expose her husband to certain death. In the morning, he would search for her remains and bury her.